HANDS OF VENGEANCE

Happy Birthday, Betty !

HANDS OF VENGEANCE

A NOVEL BY

RICHARD SAND

A LUCAS ROOK MYSTERY

DURBAN HOUSE PUBLISHING COMPANY INC.

For information address:
Durban House Publishing Company, Inc.,
7502 Greenville Avenue, Suite 500, Dallas, Texas 75231

Library of Congress Cataloging-in-Publication Data
Sand, Richard, 1943-

Hands of Vengeance/ by Richard Sand

Library of Congress Catalog Card Number: 2003105053

p. cm.

ISBN 1-930754-30-2

First Edition

10 9 8 7 6 5 4 3 2 1

Visit our Web site at
http://www.durbanhouse.com

The cover art is from the last painting by
Laurie Fabricant (1950 -2002)

For Aunt Minnie

My thanks to David Webster, Norman Santora and Jack Kroner

Lucas Rook went down the Congo River that was a New York street to the Sephora Club where his twin brother was shot to death and he had taken just revenge. Rook thought he would be part hero, but it brought him only pension money and an endless dream. His twin became a shadow calling. And a mirror too, a mirror of that mirrored death, calling for justice that was never done.

CHAPTER 1

Jackie Moore wasn't quite ready, but he flicked the outside lights off and on so they knew he was coming down. It was still dark outside, and his wife and little girl were sleeping in their small, warm rooms.

He grabbed his lunch bag, which Marie had filled the night before with two cold meat loaf sandwiches, an apple and a piece of homemade cake. Then he took some change from the kitchen bowl and flicked the lights once more. He put on his Giants jacket and went into the back room to kiss his wife and then their six-year-old, who turned inside her dream.

"Sorry I'm late," he said as he got into the smoke-filled car. Holdsworth drove one-handed with Big Earl Joost up front and Billy Gamon in the back. Billy slid over a bit so Jackie could get in.

"Time is money," Big Earl said without turning his big head.

"You think I got more time than Father Time got time, Jackie," Holdsworth added without turning around.

Billy Gamon passed the newspaper up to the front. He wasn't done reading it, but knew that he had to give the paper over to Big Earl, who rented it for a quarter from then until the ride home.

Holdsworth swung around a Chevy turning left. When he fished a Salem from his shirt, Joost moved his leg so Holdsworth could get at the lighter.

"Them nigger Knicks should rot in hell," Earl Joost said as Holdsworth lit up.

"What you expect? All them millionaire porch monkeys jumping up and down in their underwears, making all that money," Gamon said.

"It's all about the dollar," young Jackie tried.

There was a bus up ahead, but Holdsworth passed it, deftly handling the old trolley tracks that could cause a car to swerve. He glided through the light as it was turning red and checked his watch as they drove through the gates. "Three minutes to spare."

The only parking spots officially reserved at the factory were for the plant manager and the head of Human Resources. The way things worked at the Bottle House, Holdsworth got a spot close to the check-in because of his seniority.

Young Jackie Moore went up the iron steps to clock in. "Yo, boy," Big Earl called, and he made a punching motion in the air which meant for the kid to hit their cards. Jackie knew he could be written up because of that and hesitated.

"He got to take a crap, Junior," Billy Gamon yelled at the top of his lungs. They sauntered over for a cup of coffee.

Jackie's father already had nineteen years at the Bottle House. He told his son better, but there was nothing Jackie could do. The kid took his time card and the two from the top and Gamon's and clocked them all in. He changed into the navy blue pants and the shirt with the company's logo. Then young Jackie headed off to the packing floor.

The room was a huge open space with a wide conveyor belt

coming down from the ceiling and slow-moving fans that looked like airplane propellers. There were high, screened windows and two long aisles wide enough for a forklift to turn around. And stacks and stacks of boxes, filled with products to make the world thinner and more beautiful.

Arnetta Holmes sat across the conveyor belt. Like all the women in the plant, she wore a purple smock and matching head wrap. The colors went well with her brown skin and lipstick. She pursed her lips that were colored like a plum as Jackie Moore came up. "You want something hot and sweet to start your day? Nothing like a taste of cocoa to start your day."

Jackie hoped that the belt would get started. "Morning," he said.

"I never could get used to starting work when it was still dark outside," Arnetta said. "Been working here for eighteen years and this here shift every now and then, off and on. But working all night work even worser. Ruins my social life. A girl's got to have a social life. You got a social life, my fine young man?"

Jackie thought about saying something about being married, but didn't know how to do it right. Fortunately, the boxes started coming down. Arnetta waved at him and went about the job of making sure that the day's loads did not get mixed up and that all the boxes were coded right and clear. The "Slim Lite" to go down to the shipping floor and the unlabeled to come by Jackie Moore.

His job was to straighten the cartons as they came down from the palletizer and guide them to the skids at the end of the line. More often than not, it was easier to manually unload and stack them. If dented or broken boxes arrived, he was to stack them to the right.

At least three times a shift the palletizer shut down or there was a blockage jammed up the route. Sometimes Jackie Moore had to climb back up the belt and work a box loose to break the jam. A dangerous job if they didn't hear him up above or if his partner across the line didn't call in that he was going up and the conveyor belt started again.

Sometimes a box came half open, or if the belt speed got fouled, it would be like Arnetta told him happened on "I Love Lucy" with the chocolates, but he hadn't seen that. Earlier in the week, a case of fudge diet bars hit the floor and broke open. Despite the rumor that the shipping floor was videotaped, Jackie watched Arnetta sweep aside some of the bars and pick them up later.

As the sun was coming up, young Jackie had to climb on up the conveyor belt and unload the twenty cases by hand. The rest of the day went fine. Jackie Moore ate his lunch on the loading dock with two pints of iced tea he bought from the lunch truck. He tried to call home after he ate like he always did, but got a busy signal. Next month they'd get call waiting. Jackie stretched out and listened to the old man from the counting room, who played a clarinet instead of eating.

It started to rain twice on the way home. Billy Gamon got the paper back from Earl Joost, and Jackie paid Holdsworth two dollars for the roundtrip ride, which was their deal.

The carpet in Jackie Moore's parlor was white. They took great pride in that. He took his work boots off and left them in the hall. It was dinner time. Marie and Jenna were in the kitchen. His daughter was snapping green beans.

"A bean and a kiss, please," he said.

They had chicken, little potatoes with the skin on, the beans and peach ice cream.

After Jenna's bath, Marie read to her and Jackie tucked her in. He sat down in front of the TV while his wife straightened up. Jackie ate one of the candy bars Arnetta had pressed into his hand and watched ESPN until Marie came in wearing her robe, which meant it was time for bed.

While Jackie Moore was having lunch on the loading dock the next day and listening to the clarinet, he started to get sick. Big Earl and Bill Gamon gave him the business on the way home, and Holdsworth told him he better not puke in the car or he would be paying for a new interior.

When Jackie got home, Marie gave him ginger ale and when his stomach pains increased, she called Dr. Grosse down the street, who said to bring him in first thing in the morning.

The stomach pains got worse and worse. Marie drove her husband to the emergency room that night. His pain was so bad the hospital ordered a CAT scan. By the time the results came back, Jackie Moore was dead. Marie didn't know what to do or say. It was as if she had fallen into a bad dream in a different world.

Jackie's father saw to the wake and the funeral arrangements. "I wish my wife was here for you and your little girl, Marie. I wish the cancer had never taken her." Jack Moore turned away. "Only thing I can tell you is, don't let your little one grow up without a mother."

Marie Moore sat at the funeral in the white suit Jackie had gotten her for Easter. She sat motionless through the funeral service, her skin gone chalky white. "Your daddy's with the angels," she tried. "He can see us all right now, how pretty you look for him."

The little girl tried to sit up tall and to disappear at the same time. People came from the Bottle House, even some of the bosses out of respect for Jack, including Edna Charney, the head of Human Resources, and the shop steward. Holdsworth, Big Earl and Billy Gamon came from the carpool. Arnetta patted the widow's hand. There was sliced beef in gravy, pork and potato salad.

"You get pay for bereavement time, three days, Jackie's father and the union saw to that," the steward said. "And the sunshine fund. We're collecting this month's tomorrow, so I'll send it over with Jack on Wednesday."

Later that night, after Arnetta Holmes locked up her brick house on the end of the row on Tulip Street, she got severe stomach cramps.

It must be the potato salad she ate at the wake, she thought, and then was glad when the vomiting began.

Arnetta checked the clock on her bedstand. Two-thirty. "I got plenty of leave, I might as well use it." She made herself a cup of mint tea, but that didn't help. When the pains got worse, so bad that she could not stand, she dialed 911.

By the time she was seen at the Emergency Room, Arnetta Holmes was shitting blood. She died in pain as a hundred cases of poison were being trucked away from the Bottle House.

CHAPTER 2

Except for somebody who was writing him a check, there was only one lawyer Lucas Rook could sit next to for more than fifteen minutes. That lawyer was Warren Phelps.

Warren Phelps had the experience to be a top-notch defense lawyer and the innate affinity for combat. The years he did as a prosecutor with Rudy Guiliani had taught him the system and how to act like a scary prick. The most important part of being a lawyer, how to bill like the devil himself, came naturally to Phelps, which is why Rook had insisted they take the train rather than be charged for the chauffer, mileage, pro rata car insurance and lease payment and whatever else.

The Metroliner down to Philly took them a little more than an hour. The car was crowded with lobbyists on their way to Washington, brokers with step-down jobs and dozing marketers. Two high school kids with piercings sat in the next seat and acted out, the metal in their faces wagging back and forth.

Warren Phelps printed the pages from his laptop as he read them off the screen: the autopsy report, an abstract of the deposition given by Detective Salerno, and the initial suit papers filed by the child killer's estate.

The lawyer spoke only when they had both read the material. "What this is about, Lucas, is it's not a good thing to embarrass Uncle Sam. If the sister of the woman you killed, or rather who fell down the steps and broke her neck, didn't sue you, this criminal investigation doesn't happen at all."

"She just killed a cop. Burned his face off. Three, maybe four, little girls, she snatches them up and breaks their necks." Rook dropped the sheaf of papers back into the lawyer's lap.

"Maybe you should have only shot her once," Phelps said. He put the papers in his briefcase. "At the heart of this is Special Agent in Charge Robert Epps. He was the ASAC then and now he's looking somewhere up the line. The word is he's got national aspirations."

Lucas stretched out his bad leg. "Pretty boy cocksucker."

"One probably helps the other." Warren Phelps looked at his watch and then placed a call to his office. He spoke to Rook while his secretary checked another file. "So your baby killer, who happens to fall down her steps and break her neck, gets two bullets in her head and she has a sister who works for an ambulance chaser." Phelps dictated a letter to his secretary before he turned back to Rook. "Too bad the auto work dried up, Lucas. Anyway, the theory is, once the murderer fell down the steps, you had a duty to not violate her civil rights."

"My duty was to put her down."

One of the pierced kids said something, but Rook gave him a look that shut him up.

"Let's put a hold on that approach," the lawyer said. "Until we're done with our meeting with the U.S. Attorney. You good with that?"

"That's why I'm paying you four hundred dollars an hour, counselor."

"It's four fifty an hour." He looked at his platinum watch. "We got time for a drink. You want a Bloody Mary from the club car? The tomato's good for your prostate."

"So's the screwing you're giving." Rook closed his eyes and grabbed a nap sitting up. One of the finer skills acquired from thousands of hours sitting in a car waiting for somebody to come along or a door to open.

When they got to 30th Street Station, there was a line of green Victory cabs. They rode one down Market Street, past the giant clothespin sculpture. "They say they need it because the politics smells so bad around here," Phelps said. "Last time I was here, they were going to do something with that gigantic hole. Disney or something. They ever got to that?"

"Disney, a parking lot, an office building," cabbie answered. "They keep talking. Meanwhile it looks like a bomb crater." He changed lanes. "You going to Jeweler's Row, you go to Nathan's. Tell him I sent you and he gives you ten percent off."

They were twenty minutes early. "Let's grab a cup of coffee, Lucas. I want to go over everything once more before we go in. By the way, nice touch your bringing the cane with you. Injured cop. I like that."

"You're buying," Rook said. He wondered whether he should have used somebody local like Castriota, who represented the Raimondos, whose kid had gotten snatched and dead.

There was an open booth in the back of the coffee shop and they grabbed it. "My guess is they're going to have a full house up there, Lucas. Try to intimidate us. 'The United States Government versus...'."

The waiter came over. He looked like Mickey Rooney. Phelps ordered a tall hazelnut latte and a raisin pastry. Rook ordered a black coffee and a donut. "The college boys get their nuts in a knot when you clear their case, counselor."

"The Philadelphia Police Department solved these kidnappings.

Let's remember that. Detective Misher was killed in the line of duty, and you came to his aid."

"I don't need reminding."

"And you didn't know he was dead. How could you? You're not a physician. You acted to save his life and yours." He wiped some icing off his lip. "We're here to listen, Lucas. If I want you to answer, I'll nod. I will put my hands together if you should stop."

"Better than pissing on my shoe, Mr. Phelps."

There were beeping sounds from inside the attorney's pocket. He took out a gold pill box and swallowed two tablets without water. "Let's show them what lawyering is all about."

Surprisingly, the only security in the lobby of the U.S. Attorney's office was a stringy woman in a blue blazer. She pointed to the sign-in sheet and the row of visitor's tags without a word.

Warren Phelps checked his watch again. "They'll probably ice us. Have us sit at least a half hour."

"That's $200, not counting the calls you'll be making on my time. I'm sure you can live with that."

There were two waiting rooms, and they sat in the outer one for twenty minutes before a brown woman in a brown suit brought them into the next chamber. "I'm sorry for the wait. Mr. Sharkey will be with you shortly."

"'The Shark' refers to himself in the third person," Phelps said. "The Shark locked up so and so. Specializes in politicians."

"Rats chasing rats," Rook said.

The lawyer leaned over. "They're more than another half hour, I think we're going to re-scheduling this meeting."

The secretary came out. "Mr. Sharkey will see you now."

"Let's do this," Rook said.

They went through a walnut door and down a hallway. There was another waiting room with dark woodwork and a matching chair rail. There was a picture of Johnny Butler and the President on the wall.

Just as they were sitting down, a serious man in a pin-striped suit came out. He did not extend his hand. "Right this way, gentlemen. Mr. Sharkey is just finishing up."

"No staring, Lucas," Phelps said. "'The Shark' must weigh five hundred pounds."

They went into the well-appointed office. Good rugs. Leather chairs. Big windows with brass fittings. Sharkey was there and Special Agent Epps.

"Gentlemen, I am Alan Sharkey, Chief of the Criminal Division of the United States Attorney's Office for the Eastern District."

Epps finger-combed the lock of red hair off his forehead. "Mr. Rook and I have met."

"Have we?" Lucas asked.

Rook's lawyer took a small recorder from his briefcase.

Sharkey's fat swayed behind his desk. "We're getting off on the wrong foot here, counselor. The United States Attorney and the Federal Bureau of Investigation," he nodded to Epps, "consider this a very serious matter. Please set aside that recorder and do save the histrionics."

Warren Phelps brought out a yellow pad and a Mont Blanc the size of a good cigar.

"There's obstruction of justice, conspiracy and violation of the victim's civil rights," Sharkey said.

Phelps gestured with his hands, but his client ignored him.

"That's bullshit," Rook said. "And everybody in this room knows it."

The obese man's face darkened. "Counselor, another word from your client and I call the marshals."

"I appreciate how valuable your time is, Mr. Sharkey," Phelps said. "The fact Mr. Epps is here tells me that the Federal Bureau of Investigation takes this matter most seriously as well. But respectfully," he went on, "what we have is just another ambulance chaser staining the legal profession."

Epps smoothed the lime green tie that went so perfectly with his fiery hair. He started to say something, but the phone rang. It was Sharkey's private line. "You gentlemen will have to excuse me," the prosecutor said. And he turned his immense body away from them as a direction to leave.

Warren Phelps took Rook back out to the waiting room. "Trying to chill us, Lucas. He'll call us back in about twenty minutes."

"I don't think so, counselor. The look on his face when he got that call was like somebody drove off with his truck of éclairs."

Rook settled into the half-sleep that he had practiced for years. His attorney's voice woke him up. "Lawyer dies and goes to heaven. 'Saint Peter, Saint Peter,' he says. 'How can this happen? Such a young man. A man of only fifty to die so soon.' Saint Peter shakes his head and tells him, 'Fifty? According to the hours you bill your clients, you're ninety-three.'"

The pin-striped assistant escorted them in again and left. Epps was not there. Sharkey took a piece of licorice from the glass decanter on his desk. "As I was saying, the federal government is positioned to proceed in this matter involving Mr. Rook." He paused. "However, I've just been called to Washington. I'm afraid I'm going to have to defer our discussions."

"Best interests all around are served by deferring until the underlying civil case is heard, Mr. Sharkey," Phelps said.

"Perhaps," Sharkey answered. "I'll take that under advisement. Gentlemen, this meeting is now adjourned. But do expect us to revisit the matter."

Lucas wanted to tell him "bullshit" again and ask him how long ago since he saw his own pecker, but he let it pass.

"They know they have nothing," Warren Phelps said when they had gotten outside. "I'm worth every penny." He looked at his beautiful watch again and hailed a cab. "We can make the Metroliner back."

"I'll grab the next one, Warren. Going to walk around a bit."

"Suit yourself, Lucas. You're paying 'port to port' in any case. I'm actually saving your money by grabbing the early train."

The cab pulled up. "You're a prince, counselor. You really are."

Rook knew people in Philly. Inspector Zinn, Jimmy Salerno, but there was no way he was going to reach out to them with the Feds still looking at his case. Tex Cobb's was on Walnut Street, and Lucas went in for a Philly cheesesteak. There were photos on the wall of Cobb's fights with Norton, Shavers and Larry Holmes, and posters from his movies. Rook ordered a Raising Arizona and a Yuengling draft and took the next train out.

He rode back thinking of the Raimondo case. The dead little girl. The monster who had done her. Something had happened terribly wrong and he had tried to make it right. The killer was dead, but the case still called to him, like a vision of his brother up ahead.

CHAPTER 3

It had been a bag of crap couple of days for Lucas Rook. Like a bag of crap in the summer heat. His trip to Buffalo had come up empty. Two retired judges trolling for somebody to do cheap backgrounds for a casino venture in Niagara Falls. The trip to Philly with Warren Phelps cost him a fortune. The bullshit boys were squeezing him. The world was full of them, and those who made it to the top were as bad as any scumbags he had ever put away.

Rook went home. He still had not replaced the bulbs where the recessed lights were. Even over the final picture of him and his brother, Kirk, who had been gunned down in front of the Sephora Club. Although the sun was not yet completely gone, inside it was as if there had never been light at all.

He went through his dark rooms in the St. Claire Hotel to his small patio. The tiles were still warm. The air was fragrant from the flowers on the iron frames his neighbor kept and the gardenia scent the blind girl wore.

The street below changed. The traffic to a broken line, theater-goers coming in for supper, late workers getting out. Rook sat against the wall and stretched his legs. One had healed, but the other never would from the beating they had given him. They killed his brother and hurt him bad before he killed them all.

There were heavy machines starting up towards the East. Rook walked to the parapet. Two cigarettes lit in the doorway across the street as he went back inside.

It was not late enough for him to eat, and he had the book to return to Rosen, who kept his cars and sat behind the wooden desk reading with his glasses on his head.

"Suppose I was a bad guy?" Rook asked as the bay door opened.

"You are," Rosen said without looking up. "You like the book?"

Rook pulled up a metal chair. "It wasn't fast enough."

"It's not supposed to be."

Sid poured them each a drink. "You going out?"

Rook nodded and sipped the bourbon. "Business good, Sid?"

"You know how it is. Things need fixing. I fix them."

The phone rang. He didn't pick it up. "We're closed. Who's going to call after six, but to break my balls?" Rosen gave Lucas another book.

"You done, Sid?"

"I must have read *Lord Jim* a dozen times."

"Good," Rook told him.

"Good," Rosen said and he poured himself another drink.

Joe Oren's restaurant was two blocks west in what used to be a hotel lobby before the owner had changed the front. Joe was retired from off the job and had three daughters. The middle one, whose name was Jeanie, worked with him after her mother died.

"You eatin' or talkin', Rook?" Oren called from the back. "It's closing time."

Jeanie poured Lucas a cup of coffee. "He's so mean," she said.

"You working late tonight, Jeanie Oren?"

"I got a class. Two more after this and then I'm done. The chicken's good. I made it myself."

The swinging doors opened and Joe came out, a huge man with curly hair and freckles. He had a platter in one hand and a piece of pie in the other. "She sold you on the chicken, didn't she? Told you she made it, I bet. She didn't." He went back into the kitchen. "The pie's for me," he said.

Jeanie smiled. "I baked that pie." She sat across from Rook while he ate his meal.

"You gonna take her over?" Joe asked from the pass-through. "I'd appreciate that. I got another hour to do. The insurance man is coming over."

Rook left enough so she'd get three for her tip. "Problem?"

"No, Jimmie Hugues. You remember him. Did all them years in Arson till his knees went bad." He came out of the kitchen to talk to his daughter. "You wait for me inside, Mary Jean, and not the vestibule."

"Thanks, Daddy."

"See you in the vestibule," Joe said.

Jeanie put her arm inside of Rook's. She was small and smelled like soap. "We could walk. I've got time."

Rook's gait was slow. He hailed a passing cab, but it drove by. "Towel head must be going to one of his terror meetings."

"The Sikhs aren't spies, Lucas Rook. They're very respectable."

"Sure they are, Jeanie. Sure they are."

The next taxi picked them up. As it stopped in front of Goldberg Hall, she kissed Lucas lightly on the cheek. "I had a wonderful evening," she said with a little laugh.

Rook went by Oren's to tell him Mary Jean was safe, but the doors were locked and the lights were out. He went over to Sid's garage to check the doors. Then he walked the long way home.

They had replaced the doorman at the St. Claire with an automatic system, but Leo still worked the desk in the small lobby. He spit when he spoke. "Man was by. Asked for you."

"Did he leave his name or card?"

"I would have given you that, Mr. Rook."

"What he look like, Leo, tall, short, what?"

"I didn't pay him that much mind, Mr. Rook. He said he would call you later."

Lucas waited in the lobby while one of the elevators was being used for freight. Two fat men came down holding potted plants.

Rook went upstairs and unlocked the door. The mirrors in his foyer and on his bathroom door allowed him to see around the corners. The light in the closet was still on and the patio door was locked. He clicked on the wall switch with his cane.

Lucas put his .45 on the mantel next to the framed picture from the *New York Post* of him and Kirk receiving their gold shields. They had been through the academy together and rode the same blue and white. The Rook boys, the twins, who had played cowboy games and walked the beat. They dated sisters. Kirk married the smiling one, whose name was Ann.

The light on his answering machine was flashing. He poured himself a cold beer and stretched his leg. Two calls. One from Grace next door and an automated offer of a trip to Las Vegas.

Lucas picked up the messages from his office. A recording from the Police Benevolent Association reminding him to vote and a call from a man named Taighipour. Lucas erased both calls. He already had sent in his proxy for the PBA vote, and he didn't do work for anybody with Middle-Eastern names.

When things were slow, Rook wondered if maybe he should have stayed on at the pharmaceutical firm. The job was cake, the pay was icing. But then the CPA's started coming around. He could smell the books cooking.

The stockbroker who hired him next had all the money in the world, but a hundred enemies who had lost that much. No way was he going to be a full-time bodyguard. L.A. was all doped-up and lies, but he had met Scanagi, who still provided regular income. New York was where Lucas Rook belonged, and he knew it.

He started the book that Sid Rosen had given him. After another beer, he fell asleep wondering about the man who had come to see him.

C H A P T E R

Lucas Rook's office was on the part of Fifth Avenue where the
address only meant something to people from out of town. It was a
third-rate building with rag-tag tenants: a dental lab, odds and ends
of manufacturer's reps, an office for a union that represented dish-
washers and busboys. There were two Asians who would never be in
the same elevator. Next door was a photographer who never went
out.

Lucas checked the note he had written on his desk calendar.
"Appointment with Ryan, $750 balance." He had a report to drop
off and a check to pick up. Lawyers for the most part wanted you to
meet with them in their office so that they could be taking phone
calls at the same time. Either that or you met in a restaurant so they
could charge somebody for the meal.

Rook's job was done, and whether the poor slob went to jail or
not was no bother to him. Some cases he would take, some he
wouldn't. Ryan's job was some rich schmuck pinched for grabbing

at his babysitter, who was sixteen, but looked twenty-two. Rook came up with her humping everybody she could find, which would be enough to reduce the case to corrupting a minor, or make it go away altogether, since two of the humpees worked for the County. Well worth the two thousand he charged the lawyer and the four thousand the lawyer was charging the client for his investigative services.

The lawyer's office was on the second floor of a bank building in Babylon, Long Island. Two floors up was okay, and no way was he going to let a source of business see him with his cane if he could help it. Ryan's one of those general practices that handled everything that came into the door and prayed for a fat personal injury case. Lucas Rook arrived ten minutes early, a cop's habit, and waited for twenty minutes more. He was off the clock now, so he went up to the receptionist. She covered up the document she was working on.

"I'm here to pick up a check," he said.

"Mr. Ryan is in conference."

"Tell him I got his report, he got my check. What you working on? Looks important."

She went into her boss' office and came out with the envelope she exchanged with Rook. "Mr. Ryan is still with clients."

"He wishes," Lucas said. "Have a pleasant day."

Rook went back down the steps. His bad leg was stiff from all the sitting. As he came closer to the little parking lot, he heard screaming coming from the side street. He went in with his jacket open so he could reach his weapon.

And then he saw it. A girl about ten squeezed in behind a dumpster. Two pit bulls were after her. They would tear her up. The brown and white one was throwing itself against her green barricade. The brindle was jumping up with jaws that would kill her for sure.

There wasn't time to call it in, and Rook knew better than to try and pull them off. It took four rounds to put them down. One went wide and bounced into the wall across the way.

Even when the barking stopped, the girl still screamed. "Those crazy dogs are dead," Rook told her. "There aren't any dogs here anymore. I'm going to take you home. I need you to come out and help me."

Lucas walked over to bring her out, but she wasn't moving and he smelled that she had pissed herself. "It's okay," he said. "I have to go now, so you can come out and get your mom when you're ready. There are no dogs around at all."

He walked quickly back out to the street to avoid the cruiser that would be by to answer the complaints about gunfire. Anybody with half a hair up their ass would give him shit about his throwing shots. Rook crossed the street and came down the block to get his car.

He was at the traffic light when he heard somebody whistling and calling out, "Satan, Elvis." There was a yellow Hummer parked at the curb. As Lucas approached the vehicle, he could see a ham-sized hand jingling two chain leashes.

He went around the street again, coming up from the back. The big hand went back into the window and came out with a cigarette. Rook brought his black jack hard and fast. He felt the wrist shatter. Then he picked up the leashes and dropped them into the open window. "Try these on for size," he said.

Rook drove back into the City in the Avanti that had once been his brother's. He resented the fact that the fee in his pocket was going to have to cover his check to Phelps. A black sedan came up on him, then pulled around.

Lucas reached for the horn awkwardly centered in the coupe's steering wheel. The forty-year-old fiberglass car handled heavy and nose dived when he braked. But the car had been Kirk's, so he kept it for making short runs or whatever.

He was hungry for fried eggs. A habit from his years at the NYPD, eating breakfast around the clock. Sometimes to start a day's work on the graveyard shift or with a couple of beers to end the day.

Cops all had their favorite places to eat, because it was owned by a cop, like Joe's downtown, because they could get a meal "on the arm," or sometimes because it just turned out like that. Up ahead there was a place that served good eggs and crisp homefries. About six years ago Max passed on to the big luncheonette in the sky, where he was probably still cooking everything in bacon fat. His wife, Sylvia, ran the place the last time he was there.

Rook cut over and downshifted, so that the mufflers did their Vaughn Monroe. There was a cruiser up ahead making a traffic stop. Lucas knew better since he was off the job, but he swung around the corner so he could drive by in case there was trouble. The driver was a young white girl, nervously trying to find her license.

He drove by and back to Sylvia's. The place was closed. There was a smiley face hanging on the door and a sign saying, "Sorry closed early. We are opening at 7AM o'clock." Rook wondered what immigrant caste ran the place as he drove away.

CHAPTER 5

Rook wanted to get a shine, but it was raining. He had a bowl of soup at Joe's and talked about the Yankees and maybe they were the fag team in New York. Jeanie came in, but only for a minute. "Don't you eat too much," she said. "I'm going to take you dancing."

"I should live so long." Rook paid the bill and went to his office. A Latin lawyer called and said he would call back, and somebody to remind him that his liability insurance premium was due by the end of the week. Rook wrote the check and mailed from the box downstairs. Anybody who put the mail in a chute was asking for it to get fished out by some petty thief.

It was three o'clock. Rook let the first cab go by and took the second. The driver was a huge man wearing suspenders and a belt and an old style Brooklyn Dodgers hat he had on backwards. He toasted Rook with a can of grape soda. "Where to?" he asked. "Pardon the can in my hand. I love grape soda. Love it, not like it. I love it, maybe third best thing in the whole world."

"Just run me over to 40th and Lex."

"Name's Bobby," the taxi driver said. "Bobby Haak. Can you believe that? My name's Haak and I'm driving a cab. 'Hack.' Get it?"

"I got it, Bobby."

A nun fell down as the light changed. A woman in a leopardskin hat helped her up. Traffic was blocked ahead. Bobby switched lanes a couple of times before he found the flow so they could move again. Then it got slow again as they went across town.

"I'll get out here," Rook said.

Bobby toasted him with his can of grape soda and slid away to cruise for uptown fares.

Lucas went over to 40th and Lexington Avenue. He waited for almost an hour, but his accountant didn't show. He grabbed another cab and went back across town and down to Sid's.

When Rook got to the garage, Rosen was in the back working on a Dodge Durango. There were a dozen transmissions lying on the shelves.

"Always thought they look like big sea creatures, Lucas. You know, like squids. You ever pull a tranny, Rook?"

"Only when I was in vice, Sid."

Rosen stood up from his work. "Tough way to live, but you are who you are. Knew a girl for three months, maybe more, until I saw she had a cock. Little tiny one, but enough so that she wasn't getting married any day soon. Kept them little balls as smooth as Queen Ann cherries."

"That's a little more than I need to know, Sid."

Rosen found the tool he wanted, and stuck his head back under the hood. "Rush job. New customer who pays cash."

Rook went back out and walked over to the St. Claire. He took the elevator, poured himself a beer and hung his work clothes up. Then he watched an afternoon movie until he found boxing from Mexico and fell asleep.

When he awoke, he took a shower and went to his kitchenette to scramble a couple of eggs. He put mustard on them. His brother always laughed at that. "The ketchup and mustard twins," Kirk and him were called for awhile at their first command. That was at the Two-Five. Wisnewski ran the house, but he was long gone.

Lucas poured himself a tomato juice and went onto his patio. The blind girl from next door was outside smoking. Grace had an incredible body.

"Still waiting for you to cuff me," she said.

"Still waiting for you to do something bad, Grace."

His phone rang and he went in to get it. It was the Latin lawyer transferred over from the office line. Cuban, he figured from the accent.

"You're a hard man to reach, Lucas Rook."

"Business is good. You wanted a call back, you'd leave a number."

"Fair enough. I am Felix Gavilan, Attorney at law. Calling from Atlanta. May I ask what your rate is?"

Rook doodled on a napkin. "Depends on the case. Depends on who's paying. Sometimes by the day. Sometimes by the week. You letting your fingers do the walking?"

"You came highly recommended, the Ballem case." The lawyer paused, inviting a comment.

"I don't discuss my clients or my cases." Lucas put a half a bagel in the toaster. "You want to tell me what this is about, we can talk business. You want to meet, nothing happens, I eat my time. We reach an agreement, my time is on the clock."

Gavilan's secretary buzzed him. "Lunch tomorrow?" he asked when he got back on. "I've got a client who wishes to surrender."

"For what?"

"It's a narcotics case. A dentist."

Rook buttered his bagel. "We got a 'Larry Lavin' here?"

"Excuse me."

"Eighty-six co-conspirators," Rook said. "A regular cartel. Uncle gave him forty years."

Another call came through. Gavilan told his secretary to take a message. "Nothing like that."

"Then he's shopping, counselor."

"Precisely. He'd like to surrender to the county authorities in West Chester. You're interested, it's seventy-five dollars an hour, seven hundred fifty dollar retainer."

"You're putting me in the middle, the state, the DEA." Lucas poured himself another cup of coffee. "Plus I'm cheaper than if you hire West Chester co-counsel. A hundred an hour and the retainer is twelve fifty, non-refundable."

"The expenses are yours, Mr. Rook. The clock starts tomorrow at six at DiLullo's in Tarreytown. And by the way, I'm his brother-in-law."

Lucas kept all his files on index cards. He wrote out some notes and banded a stack of cards, which he put under "G." Then he poured himself a beer and read the paper, folding it twice longwise so none of his surroundings were hidden. Safety first. Like keeping one leg out of your pants when you were taking a dump.

There was an article about a software pirate getting sixty months federal time. Techno-crime was a good field if he could get the business, partner up with that curly-haired guy used to work at the A.G.'s office. There was a two-page story on the latest investigation at Local 36. New regime meant new thieves. That's the way the world went, and it kept him working.

❦   ❦   ❦

Rook drove out to West Chester County to meet Attorney Gavilan and get the job running. The retainer would be good. He needed to get a copier for the office.

He only had one ongoing commercial account. Scanagi Enterprises was the domestic arm of a French conglomerate that paid him $3,000 a month to do background checks and light security ever since he had gotten Paul Scanagi out of a vice problem in LA. Other than that, it was getting harder and harder to secure commercial work. Big companies like Pinkerton touting all their electronics were now going after smaller jobs. At the same time, more and more cops were going on retirement and having to supplement their income. Everybody had a computer. Skip-tracing and work like that was non-existent.

Rook rolled up on the Tarreytown restaurant fifteen minutes early. Cops always showed up early so there were no surprises. DiLullo's had been there for years. When he was on the job, he had been out there with Blackburn to bring in Izzy the Hat. Always had his fedora and a bad attitude on. Blackburn jacks Izzy and his hat comes off, his hair with it. The hat had just the fringes of a hairpiece sewn in.

The restaurant was red sandstone with a large portico in the front. It had a large parking lot in the rear and slant parking on the left side. The adjoining streets had been made one-way. Somebody knew somebody. On the right were a gazebo, concrete benches and a wishing well that had been capped, probably for liability reasons.

Lucas swung around a second time and parked against the side of the place. He went in without a word. The restaurant had been done over. The exit was off the hall to the restrooms and the phone. He slipped back outside.

A silver Mercedes pulled up. There were two Latin men in it, a short one driving and a tall one leaning against the window. He got out first. They were both dressed GQ and walked soft. When the driver tipped the valet, he showed a Rolly like a clock radio.

Rook went back inside and introduced himself. Gavilan's hair was perfectly black. His skin was perfectly smooth. When he extended his small hand he showed cuff links with the scales of justice in gold and diamonds.

"Mr. Rook, I take it."

Lucas nodded.

"And this is my paralegal, Miguel."

Miguel smiled perfectly with perfect caps.

The hostess came over. A new blonde with too much perfume. "Your server will be right with you."

"Server sounds so stilted to me," the lawyer said as they sat down. "But ever since that Third Circuit case eroding *Farangher and Ellerth...*"

"The sexual harassment cases."

"Very good, Mr. Rook. The defendants never think they're wrong and they always pay." Gavilan nodded to his assistant. "Which reminds me..."

Miguel reached into his pocket for the envelope. Rook could see a suede holster and a chromed semi-automatic.

"Your retainer, Mr. Rook. There's a two-page agreement. It's standard, confirming your status as a fully licensed, independent contractor. You pay your own taxes and maintain your own insurance. Please do add my office as an additional insured."

Miguel's hands were thin and his eyes were cold. Rook took the envelope. "Cash in, check out, counselor?"

Miguel started to speak, but Gavilan waved him off. "My check is good. I have a reputation to protect."

The waitress came over, a slightly shorter version of the hostess and wearing the same overwhelming scent. Gavilan ordered two cosmopolitans. Rook had a Miller Lite. When he put the envelope inside his sportscoat, Miguel wasn't watching at all.

"So fill me in, counselor. We having a fourth for lunch?"

Gavilan adjusted his shirtcuffs again. "I'm afraid not. Dr. Alterstein's not handling this well at all."

"What's he looking at?"

"Notwithstanding his own paranoia that he's going to get executed, he does what I tell him, he might not even go away."

The drinks came. Rook waited for the waitress to leave.

"The good doctor's behavior completely local?"

"I believe it is. But you can confirm that. In any case, I think he's certainly going to have a problem with the state about his license. I'm looking to keep that down to a suspension. I may need your services there too, statements from his patients, a complete background."

Rook sipped his beer. "You said you're his brother-in-law, Mr. Gavilan?"

"He's married to my sister. Beautiful woman."

Miguel said something into his pink cocktail.

The lawyer went on. "The best plastic surgery money can buy. That's where the trouble comes from."

"The painkillers."

"Right. Percocet to Oxycontin. She takes them. She loves me. She needs them. Then she falls in love with coke. He's writing the scripts. Then he's selling them."

Rook filled his glass. "And when this is all done, she's going to leave him."

"Very astute, Mr. Rook. My sister, the lovely Cielto, she calls herself 'Sky.' Sky Alterstein, she's going to blame him for everything."

The lawyer's cell rang. The call was brief. He sent Miguel for the waitress and finished his drink. "Thank heavens I set big retainers, Mr. Rook. The good dentist just shot himself to death in their breakfast room." He looked at his enormous watch. "Will you be joining us for lunch?"

Lucas finished his beer. "I'll be running along, Mr. Gavilan. I trust you won't be stopping payment on that check."

"Certainly not. That would be unprofessional."

"Not smart either," Rook said.

Rook checked the envelope more thoroughly in the hallway. If something wasn't right, Lucy and Ricky were going to have a problem. Inside was the two-page agreement on high quality paper and the check. He left by the side door. Now there were two silver Mercedes. Rook took down the license plates, which were both New York, and drove back in. He rode with the windows down and the radio on.

About halfway to the City, he stopped for gas. He was hungry, but no way was he going to sit with the oiled-up lawyer and his Latin lover if he didn't have to.

Lucas checked the time. Chinese would be good. Bill Young's place always had a seat for a cop on or off the job and especially for Rook, who had stopped a hold-up in there. He went over. Bill was in the back and came out when his wife called in who it was.

"I'll make you something special," he said.

Rook knew not to argue. "Just no fish with heads on."

"No problem," Bill said. "Stacy, pour my good friend here a Tsing Tao."

The cold beer came. The best in the world, except maybe for Kirin, but no way were you going to get a Jap beer in a Chinese restaurant.

The meal was just what he needed. Lucas paid the bill in full, but left no tip, an arrangement they'd had for years. The beer was on the house.

Then he went home. There were two calls on his message machine, both from overseas. The phone rang again. It was Paul Scanagi. "Sorry I don't have time for foreplay, Lucas."

"Just give it to me."

"Stateside business is going into Chapter 11. Our counsel tells me there's no way your retainer was going to make it by the Creditors' Committee or the bankruptcy trustee."

"Is that that sound of three large times twelve going down the crapper, Paul?"

"I guess it is, Lucas. I'll try and throw some business your way."

"Grease me up first, next time," Rook said, as he hung up. Maybe it was the loss of two clients or maybe the Chinese food, but Rook could not sleep.

He went out onto his small patio, then came inside again and went down into the street. The cost of his apartment in the St. Claire was capped by New York's World War II rent control. The office at 166th was cheap. He had no staff. And his pension check came monthly from his service-related disability retirement. Somebody at the top had seen to it that the leg injury suffered at the hands of Kirk's murderers had been designated as job-related. Sometimes Rook wished that wasn't so.

Lucas Rook walked the streets, his cane touching the sidewalk as much for company as for support. Losing the clients meant there was less for him to do, and that meant more to think about. He walked almost to Sheridan Square, then started back, thinking unexpectedly of that night he heard that Kirk was shot and he came rushing down the West Side Highway, his sirens screaming.

When he got back to the St. Claire he had a couple of beers too many. Rook dreamed over and over again of a pale shadow in an empty room.

CHAPTER 6

Webster Clark knew about death. He had smelled its smells and heard its screams in Vietnam. He had watched it like a hundred TV shows and dealt it out like a game of cards. He knew how to add it up so it made sense. Now it was eating him up. The catheter inside his pants. Taking Percocets like peppermints. Years of life falling apart, leaving nothing inside but rot.

The sun was caught inside the branches of a tree as he got up. He put on his wire-rims and made himself a cup of herbal tea. The neighbor's orange cat had started coming up to kill the morning birds since he buried their spaniel in the yard. He rapped on the window to chase the predator away.

Virginia was still asleep when Web went back in to say goodbye. He kissed the corner of her mouth, which made her smile, and went to work.

Down Greenhill Road to Crescent and on to the Southway. Then 295 to U.S. 50, which got backed up by glare and poor design.

Greenbelt, Maryland was one of three communities built by Roosevelt's New Deal. They had planned someday to be in Greenhills, Ohio, Greendale, Wisconsin, and home on the same day. And always to be together, the two of them, sitting with some grace on their porch that wrapped around to the poplar trees. Having wine as the night came in or iced tea in the summertime. If his cancer or whatever didn't kill him first.

The Pendle Institute was founded in 1965 to do research, assessment, and resolution. Now it offered a respected quarterly, an online newsletter and seminars on subjects such as Domestic Preparedness and Risk Assessment of Asymmetric Threats. Additionally, the Institute implemented various projects of applied theory, particularly in Consequence Management.

The establishment of the so-called "Trilogy," the FBI, CIA, and Homeland Security, had actually increased the activity at the Institute. The alleged cooperation of the three agencies made a "backroom" all the more attractive when there was dirty work to do.

The Institute was in a three-story brick building. It had white colonial trim and a walled courtyard. There were brick walkways going out in three directions, and what had been the stables had been converted to meeting rooms. He drove by the coffee shop on the corner and then around again to the parking lot in the rear.

Joyce was coming down the back stairs as he started up, and Web stood aside to let her pass. "You look well," he said.

"Thank you. I like your bow tie. I tried one for Don, but he never could get the hang of it." She smiled and went down the hall to the copy room.

Webster Clark went up the narrow steps to the bathroom to check his urine bag and take two Percocets. The pain was coming on. He washed his face and went into his office and closed the door.

Web had been working at the Institute for fifteen years and was well regarded in his field. Now the disease, the pain and medication were weakening him. He worried whether he would be able to earn the maximum employee benefits available to him and to do what needed to be done.

He made himself a cup of tea and leaned back in his chair until the drugs kicked in. There was a picture on his desk of Virginia and him in fishing hats, and another with their dog that died last year. On the wall was an old photo of him in jungle gear and an autographed picture of Billy Conn. The Wilton rug had come from home.

Clark reviewed the file for his eight-thirty meeting. It was the last one he'd be working on, but as with all the rest, he knew the case and the background material thoroughly. He scanned the file in his computer and then his own encrypted notes in preparation for his meeting with the Director.

At twenty after eight, Joyce buzzed Clark to say that Dr. Pransky was ready for him. Pransky had been at the Institute since its inception, bringing his Ph.D. from Northwestern and twenty-three years at the CIA. He had a beard that looked like Santa Claus', but a hard face. He was at his triangular desk, looking through files and sketching a landscape design around the notes he had made.

"Come in, Webster. Come in. Time for some more 'spring tonic' to purge the system." He drew the castor bean plant with its alternating leaves. "Christ, I've seen the *Ricinus Communis* growing in a planter outside the Smithsonian. So common, so accessible. A WMD growing by the roadside."

"The poison shows up, we get rid of the poisoners," Clark said. "Kenneth Olsen was grabbed up in Spokane last year. James Glick in Tampa. Maynard Campbell…"

The Director put his pencil down. "A particle of ricin the size of a grain of salt can kill a man, Webster. But nobody's come up with a delivery system to make it amount to anything, not even the esteemed Professor Akdid at Baghdad University or everybody's favorite Iraqi, the lovely Dr. Germ. And everybody's been trying since the 'W' bomb in World War I.

"In reality, this ricin thing is nothing more than pig waste," Pransky went on. "Except that the press whores make it sound like the end of the world. Arrests in Barcelona of food workers who may have been part of an Algerian group who may have been attached to Ansar al-Islam in Northeastern Iraq and may have been working with Bin Laden and may have been planning to put something in the food at a British military base that might have been ricin." He started to draw again, then stopped. "Christ, you'd think it was 1915 again and we were facing the chlorine gas at Ypres."

"Pig waste that needs cleaning up," Clark said. "One gram can kill 50,000 people, and there's no known antidote. The antigen, MicroVax, is still in trials. And beside that, ricin is essentially undetectable, before and after delivery."

"Of course, Web, of course. Pig waste, fig paste. Your assessment is first rate as usual." He ran his hand over the memory of his crew cut. "It does get more complicated in our casualty-averse democracy. You'll keep me informed of your progress, Webster, and if there's any complications."

Clark stared at the purple dot on Pransky's lip, wondering if like the spot on his bladder, it would spread and eat the Director up. "I'm sorry that I didn't make the opening of your show. I understand you won a prize. Virginia and I planned to go, but that thunderstorm came up out of nowhere."

Pransky smiled. "Lots of Prussian Blue on my palate," he said. An inside joke. Ferric hexacyanoferrate was a painter's pigment and the recommended treatment for radiation from a dirty bomb.

Webster Clark went back to his office. He knew what his job was and what he was going to do. The Director referred to ricin as fig paste. Fig paste from Agatha Christie's *The Home of Lurking Death*. Ricin was easily extracted from castor oil beans. It was six thousand times more deadly than the venom of a rattlesnake. In Latin, it was called *Palma Christ* – "The Palms of Christ." The irony of that was never lost on him.

Webster was an expert on ricin. Herodotus wrote about the castor bean, the Egyptians buried it in their tombs. Castor oil was manufactured throughout the world from millions of tons of beans, but the process had been banned in the United States since the 1970's. The plants grew naturally throughout the temperate parts of the United States and were widely cultivated on decks and patios.

He also was an expert in the art of using poison as a weapon of politics. Dahm Y'Israel Nokeam trying to avenge the Holocaust with arsenic in 1946. The Holocaust survivors poisoned thousands of SS prisoners by lacing pumpernickel with arsenic. More than 4,000 were sickened, almost 1,000 paralyzed or dead. RISE's plan a quarter of a century later to poison Chicago water supplies with typhoid and diphtheria. The Covenant Sword and Arm using cyanide to erase all non-Aryans in 1986. The Rajneeshees poisoning salad bars in Chicago. The Aum poisoning the Tokyo subways in 1995 with sarin gas, having gone undetected in twenty other attacks.

The Minnesota Patriots Council made their own history in 1995. Four members of the MPC planned to use ricin for revenge against the federal government because one of them was served with papers for tax evasion. When the Bureau penetrated the Council, they discovered that the poison delivery system, which utilized hand lotion, was totally useless.

That same year, Webster Clark learned a lot about poison from Thomas Lavy. Thomas Lavy was arrested in his cabin in the Ozarks. The Arkansas chicken farmer, turned terrorist, was caught trying to smuggle 130 grams of ricin in from Canada along with 20,000 rounds of ammunition and $80,000. His explanation was that he was interested in the method employed by Montana shepherds to kill coyotes.

Mr. Lavy's prosecution under the Biological Weapons Anti-Terrorism Act and a media frenzy were avoided when he was found hanged in his cell. Clark said nothing before he strung him up.

Ricin was a virulent bioweapon, a deadly poison, readily made from the hundreds of thousands of tons of castor seed waste produced overseas or from the common domestic plant. There had been six deaths in one New York county confirmed to be from ricin poisoning. But that was not the threat Webster Clark was dealing with on this assignment.

The threat was the poisoning of the Nation's sense of security. There would be hundreds of hours of prime time nightmares. The press would turn every umbrella into the one that delivered ricin pellets to Markov and Kostov thirty years ago. There would be another terror shadowing us. Another horror to haunt our sleep.

All of this when the actual casualties would be no more than an auto crash on an icy road. It would be another paralyzing anthrax scare. That was the real poison, and Webster Clark knew it was as lethal as the cancer that was killing him.

C H A P T E R 7

When Lucas Rook saw that the elevators were down again at his office building, he went around the corner to get the shine that had been rained out.

"Hop on up, Mr. Rook," Jimbo Turner said. "Your leg must be acting up the way you're walking."

"How ya doin', Jimbo?"

"Not bad for a half-deaf, diabetic, white shineman." He ran his fingers across Rook's shoes.

"Can always tell when you been driving a lot. The tips all raw the way they is. You go to Jersey, bring me back some of that sweet corn." He rolled up the pants cuffs. "How you want these?"

"Cordovan is good," Rook said.

The shineman lit a match and set it into the can of polish. While it softened up, he applied the wash to each shoe and wiped them down. Then he rubbed the cordovan in with his fingertips.

Rook took the newspaper that Jimbo had bought for his clientele.

"That new boy with the Mets got himself busted already. Got him speeding with a bag of blow in his car, Lucas Rook. First thing they do when they come over here from Mexico or whatever is pick up the bad habits." Jimbo rubbed the polish in. "Cocaine, make a man insane." He took a toothbrush from his denim apron and ran it along the edges of the shoes.

Rook turned to the sports page. "The Golden Boy going to make another run, Jimbo."

"Takes too many punches. Ain't goin' to be no pretty boy no more. Lots of me don't work, but my face still pretty. My sugar diabetes didn't get to me, I'd fight him for the million bucks they pay." He clicked the backs of his brushes together.

"What you hear, Jimbo? What you know?"

"Your competition been by, Womack smelling all like a pimp the way he do. Man gives me his new card, matter of fact a couple of them, got one of them raised seals on it. Tells me one hand washes the other. I tell him I wash my own hands. Don't need to do business with him."

A man went by with a parrot on his arm.

"Womack, he tells me was a gold shield over in Hackensack before he got his license, Lucas Rook. But whether that's true or not, he still running his accident cases for them PI lawyers."

"Buying up the 48's and selling them to the shysters, Jimbo. Better than what he used to do, which was selling babies."

Jimbo Turner snapped the rag. "Over at McCauley's, young punk comes in to rob the place and McCauley, he puts a pool cue through the asshole's eye. Womack says the asshole's going to make a million. You pinched his sorry self, didn't you, Rook?"

"That I did. Caught Womack salting the mine with this rich old widow lived at the Dakota. Took her for $7,500 to find her Siamese cat, which had gotten ran over by the crosstown."

The bootblack tapped the bottom of Rook's shoes, meaning he was done, and then offered his shoulder for support as Lucas got down. Jimbo Turner used his whisk broom like a musician and took Rook's five with a little salute.

"You see a man around asking for me, Jimbo, you let me know."

"I'll call you up in a heartbeat."

"You take care, Mr. Turner," Rook said. "I'll see you the end of the week."

Jimbo Turner gave a little bow.

When Rook got back to 166 Fifth, the elevator was still down. The girls from the insurance office were outside smoking.

"Smoking's hazardous to your health, ladies," Lucas told them.

The one with the braids stuck her tongue out at him. "That's how I like it," she said.

Rook shook his head and went to find the super, who was in his apartment in the basement. "I'm waiting for repair," he said without opening the door. "How long that going to be?"

"Soon, soon. Meanwhile I'm busy."

"Don't forget to wash your pecker when you're done."

"Shut your pie hole, Rook," the super yelled, but Lucas had gone back upstairs.

One of the elevators was running and there was a line in front of it. Rook saw a sweating man and the one from the dental supply with the nicotine-stained fingers. A salt and pepper couple trying not to hold hands got on, and the Japanese, looking only straight ahead.

It took two carloads to get Rook. He rode up with the smoking girls and an old lady with a postcard in her hand.

When he got to his office, there was a well-dressed woman at his door. She wore her hair in a bun and was holding an expensive black coat over her arm. Her suit was elegant.

"Mr. Rook," she said. "I hope you're worth the trip."

"I hope so too," he said as he opened the door.

"My name is Helena Politte. May I have a glass of water?"

Rook showed her to one of the two client chairs and took a bottle of water from the fridge. "Do we have an appointment, Mrs. Politte?" He filled a styrofoam cup and passed it to her.

"No we do not, but I am interested in discussing your services. I'm sorry for the lack of advance notice, but I just arrived. I'm staying at the Towers." She sipped the water. "You were referred to me by Mr. Scanagi. My husband had business with him. Of course, I checked you in the Regency Directory."

"Of course."

"And I may be interviewing someone else."

Rook nodded. He would be interviewing her too, her ability and willingness to pay, her emotional state, the case itself. "How can I help you?" He took a legal pad out of his desk.

"Mr. Scanagi tells me that you specialize in industrial matters."

Thanks for the lie, Paul, he thought. "I've had a number of complex matters in that area. What particular type of industrial matter are we speaking about?"

She stared at the wall behind him. He waited for her to come around.

"I'm sorry, Mr. Rook," she said. "I left quite early."

"How can I help you?"

Mrs. Politte opened her handbag and took out her checkbook. "We, Politte Industries, may have what they tell me is called 'violence in the workplace.' Some of our employees at one of the plants have died, perhaps from product tampering, although there's been no untoward cause of death established. At first, Listeria was suspected, but we're quite clean. My attorneys suggested Pinkerton or Wackenhut, but Mr. Scanagi recommended you and my husband trusted him." She stared at the wall again.

"Do you suspect a competitor?"

"We have none really for what we do. Ours is a niche industry. We manufacture private label diet aids."

"Has there been any labor discord, Mrs. Politte?"

"No, our contracts are negotiated quite amicably." She finished the water.

Lucas made some notes. "Have there been any associated fatalities outside of the workplace, Mrs. Politte?"

"That I would not know. I do not have much interaction with the local community."

"May I ask why you think the deaths were the result of product tampering?"

"I do not. My attorneys tell me if the deaths are caused by a third party, such as by product tampering, there's no insurance coverage. That determination is the reason I require your services." She produced her pen. "I trust you are licensed and bonded."

"And insured, Mrs. Politte. My rate is $125 per hour, plus expenses. I require a twenty-five-hundred-dollar retainer."

She wrote the check. "My attorneys are expecting you. They have a local office on Park Avenue."

Mrs. Politte got up and put her coat on. She handed Rook the check and the law firm's card. "And please do wear a tie," she said as she let herself out.

CHAPTER 8

The New York Office of Kipps, Wetherill and Hobbes occupied the second floor of a Park Avenue building. Like their other offices in Boston, Washington D.C., and London, it was appointed with understated luxury. The rugs were deep, the furniture old, and the paintings of dead industrialists.

"May I help you?" the receptionist asked.

"I have an appointment with Mr. Shipley."

"Oh, yes, Mr. Rook. Mr. Shipley is running a little late. May I offer you some coffee or tea?"

As he waited for his audience with Mrs. Politte's lawyer, Lucas read the firm brochure. "Kipps, Wetherill and Hobbes" was more than two hundred years old and considered itself the nation's "oldest corporate law specialist." From the bios, he saw that there was a Mr. Kipps in Boston and a Wetherill in D.C. Family solidarity or the fountain of youth.

This particular office had sixteen lawyers. Spencer Shipley appeared to be the second in line. Good credentials, Rook thought. Admitted to both the New York and DC bars and an MBA from Wharton.

In forty minutes a man with wavy black hair combed properly to the side came out to greet Lucas. He wore a tweed suit, French cuffed shirt and a club tie. "Mr. Rook," he said.

Rook extended his hand. "Mr. Shipley," he said.

"I'm sorry. I'm Arthur Eck, his assistant. Mr. Shipley is this way."

They went through brass-handled doors and down a hall to another set of doors. Eck knocked and took Rook in. Shipley was on the phone. He gestured for his assistant to leave and Lucas to sit.

"Certainly, certainly," Spencer Shipley continued. "But we are planning to settle tomorrow with or without your cooperation. If this lis pendis is not removed by 9:00 AM tomorrow, we'll be in for equitable relief and counsel fees by 10." He made a memo on his computer. "Right, right. We can escrow enough to cover your client's claim and your fee. I'll see you tomorrow at the settlement table."

"Sorry not to get up, Mr. Rook. My disability's quite an annoyance," he said, leaning a bit to shake hands. "Arthur tells me you have met Mrs. Politte."

"Mrs. Politte retained me. She said you'd fill me in."

Shipley reached for the decanters on his left. "Would you like a glass of water? Sparkling, still, or iced?"

"Still is fine."

The lawyer poured them each a glass of Evian. "I still can't get over it. Selling water in a bottle. I hear they sell oxygen in Tokyo." He put two ice cubes in his glass. "Yes, the insurance coverage problem. Quite a minefield, coverage issues, but Mr. Scanagi says you're perfectly well-suited."

Shipley opened the file on his desk and retrieved an original and copy of bluebacked agreements. "Feel free to have your attorney review this employment agreement and forward me a redlined copy."

Rook scanned the twenty-eight pages. "I told Mrs. Politte my rates. She gave me the retainer. No way I sign a twenty-eight-page agreement about anything." He handed back the contract. "Also I bill monthly, not quarterly, and your threshold for reimbursement of expenses is too high."

Shipley picked up his intercom and called for Eve to come in with her book. She sat in the chair next to Rook and crossed her long legs. The lawyer dictated a two-page agreement, and she left.

"Fantastic, isn't she?" the lawyer smiled.

"What can you tell me, counselor?"

Spencer Shipley arched his back. "Your services are being retained on account of the insurance issue." He rolled his pen around like he was doing a magic trick. "Neither of Mrs. Politte's relevant insurance policies, workers' compensation, or general liability cover intentional acts by a third person. There have been some deaths in the workplace. Both insurance carriers have sent 'Reservation of Rights' letters. They are reserving the right to pay any claims, but will at this point pay for defense litigation. They will allow us to represent her company at reduced rates and to secure her own investigator.

"Additionally, as with all policies written after 9/11/01, Mrs. Politte's coverage contains a 'terrorism exclusion,' which means if the deaths are caused by terrorism, foreign or domestic, they pay nothing, including attorney's fees." Shipley rolled his neck. "We are retaining you on Mrs. Politte's behalf to conduct a diligent investigation as to the cause of the deaths."

"And depending upon my conclusions, you'll present them to the insurance carrier or not." Rook said, "Have any claims been filed yet, counselor?"

Shipley nodded. "From our perspective they have not. We've received no letter of representations on behalf of any of the decedents."

"Have there been any investigations by the local police or other authorities?"

"There have not, Mr. Rook. This, it appears, is a matter that only concerns the Regal and Union Insurance Carriers."

"And dictates your firm's billing rate, if I am correct, Mr. Shipley. If the deaths are caused by terrorism, the insurance carriers will not pay and Mrs. Politte will be billed at your usual rates."

"That is possible." Spencer Shipley refilled his water glass. "We hope we can rely on your professionalism in this matter."

"You can," Rook said. "And so can Mrs. Politte."

Shipley handed Rook a manila envelope. "Mrs. Politte's factory manufactures and labels diet aids. There's ample information inside. I expect that you will be reporting to Mr. Eck weekly or more frequently, if anything significant develops."

"I'm working for your client, Mr. Shipley. I report to the person who writes the checks."

Shipley handed over a document signed by Mrs. Politte. "This authorizes you to do as I ask. Report to Mr. Eck. Send your billing to the firm. Any questions?"

"I'll need confirmation of the billing agreement from Mrs. Politte. She has already paid my retainer."

"That will be provided, of course."

Spencer Shipley buzzed Eck to show Lucas out.

Rook was on the clock from the moment that meeting began, so he got a receipt from the cabby who dropped him off at Joe Oren's. Sam was working behind the counter and came over to the booth to take his order.

"What you having, Detective?"

"Just coffee, Sam."

"That's good, cause Joe throwed his back out."

Lucas opened the envelope Shipley had given him. There was more information than he expected, but at their hourly rates, he wasn't surprised.

Oneonta, New York was 202 miles from Manhattan. "The City

of the Hills" equidistant between Binghamton and Albany. Located on the Susquehanna River and Route 88 at the foothills of the Catskill Mountains. Population 14,000. Home of Hartwick College and SUNY Oneonta and the Oneonta Tigers baseball team. Main Street features an old fashioned bandstand and "century old atmosphere." The other major businesses were F N Burt Company and Astrocam Electronics. Mrs. Politte's company was quaintly referred to as "The Bottle House" because it occupied the old Abbott's Dairy, which had a landmark concrete milk bottle 50 feet high. Rook's local contact was Peter Henn at the law firm of Van Patton and Henn.

Sam brought a bowl of soup. "Veggie gumbo," he said. "Last night's veggie and tonight's gumbo. On the house."

"Don't be givin' away my secrets," Joe called from the back. He came out, listing to the side.

"I thought you were out," Lucas said.

"Soon as the Flexeril hits, I'm good. Put some frozen peas on my back, I'm good to go. Got a girl at NYU, you know. Costs a fortune."

"She's a good girl."

"That she is, Lucas. But she can manipulate you around. She gets me good."

"Like she should," Sam called from the kitchen.

Rook ate the soup and went over to the garage. The place was locked and the alarm was armed. Lucas left a note to lube his Crown Vic and took Kirk's Avanti out.

He rode with the windows down to watch the City breathe and breed. Podiatrists' wives coming in to shop. Children working in basement rooms. He went by crimes being planned and carried out. Racks of clothes being rolled away. Spoiled fish sold fresh. Up inside the glass buildings, robbers were wearing silk.

Lucas went to buy a pair of shoes, but Luben's was closed. He stopped at Jerry John's, then cruised by Sutton Place, where rich folks lived inside of tombs. Webster Clark followed him three cars behind.

CHAPTER 9

Grace came out of Rook's building as he was going in. Other than her dark glasses, no one would suspect her blindness.

"They're taking me away, Lucas."

"Are you alright?" he asked.

"Please water my lovelies," she said.

A stretch limo pulled up and she got in. Lucas went upstairs. He put his .45 on the mantel and read the mail, three solicitations to join a dating service, a reminder that his PI bond was due for renewal, a catalog from John Jay College for continuing education, and a letter from Catherine Wren.

He opened Catherine's letter. They had been together for almost two years, and he hadn't heard from her since that night at her place when she said she couldn't stand his "private justice" anymore.

Dear Lucas, I cannot say I haven't missed you. Nor can I say I haven't been glad at the absence of drama. Feeling safer and unsafe at the same time. I'm running more and cooking less. If you ever decide to teach school or sell insurance, I'll be waiting. Love, Cat.

He poured himself a Sam Adams and listened to his phone messages. A call from Sid that he was going out to see his wife and a song from Grace to water her plants. He checked his answering machine at the office. Dick Slavitt to refer a matter, the Korean from upstairs, and Mrs. Politte confirming that he should bill to the lawyers.

Rook went in to the back room and cleaned his ankle piece. He wrapped the .38 well and put it in a Whitman's chocolate box. Then he went out onto his patio and drank another beer, listening to the street sounds and watching a hawk circle in the sundown.

Lucas was in bed when he realized he had forgotten Grace's plants. He went outside again and climbed over the low wall between their patios and watered her flowers in the dark.

In the morning Rook walked over to Oren's for coffee and picked up his Crown Victoria, the universal cop car and good on the road despite the way the gas tanks could go up. Sid had put a shield around the tank long before Ford admitted their twenty-year-old problem.

Lucas ran the Palisades Parkway to the Thruway. The Garden State had more toll stops than a whore on a busy night. It was slightly more than a hundred miles on Route 17. He listened to the assholes on talk radio and then oldies. Route 88, took him right into the heart of Oneonta. He'd seen the mixture of quaint and rundown in lots of towns trying to replace industrial jobs with tourism. It never worked. Oneonta, home of the Soccer Hall of Fame and empty factories.

Van Patton and Henn was in a tan stucco property. In the front was a real estate company and title insurance business. There was no receptionist. A man with big ears and a moustache came out of one of the back offices.

Lucas gave him his card with the chess piece on it. "I'm looking for Peter Henn."

"You found him. People say I look like Clark Gable, though." The phone on the front desk rang and Henn picked it up. "American Title," he said and jotted down some information.

"Let's go into my office, Mr. Rook," Henn said. "Busy, busy, especially with my secretary out. Hard worker, well-liked, and the bluest-blue eyes, but her kid gets one of his ear aches, she's out." He motioned Rook to sit. "Coffee?"

"Coffee's good."

"It's not half-bad. Must say so myself. Better than instant, but not as good as hers. She makes a terrific cup of coffee, my Lucille does. They told me to expect you. We've worked together before. I mean me and Eck, not the whole firm."

"Van Patton?" Rook asked, to slow him down.

Henn was talking over his shoulder as he walked back to his office. "I'm the firm, I mean Mr. Patton is still deceased. As still as still can be."

Rook sat down in one of the vinyl chairs. "I'm on the clock here, counselor."

"Right. Right. I guess I should get to it. Good idea, as good as maybe cutting back the coffee to maybe ten to twelve cups. I guess I should, but they say drinking seven cups a day prevents diabetes."

Lucas stretched out his leg and waited for the lawyer to get to the point. Peter Henn retrieved a manila file from the corner of the desk. "Right. Right," he said. "You're the investigator. Some trouble out at the plant, the 'Bottle House' we call it. I don't see it, but Mrs. Politte seems to and her law firm in Manhattan does, so…"

"See what, counselor?" Henn answered as he thumbed through the file. "I can smell something when it's going on. I used to work in the prosecutor's office. Some folks at the factory got sick and died, which is a shame. But it's a coincidence, that's all."

Lucas took the narrow reporter's pad from inside his sportcoat. "I don't believe in coincidences. Tell me about the Bottle House.

Any other problems out there?"

"H.R. Director, Human Resources. You're going to meet with her, Edna Charney. She plays for the other team."

"Meaning what?"

"Meaning she's 'that way.' Bats from the wrong side of the plate. Lock up your sister. She's a lesbo with an attitude. She says she got some evidence though."

"What's that, Peter?"

"Videotape of stealing on the packing floor." Henn handed over a two-page report. "Client of mine was going to make an unemployment claim."

Rook scanned it. "I'd like a copy of the tape."

"I don't have that. But from my experience…"

"In the Prosecutor's Office."

"I say that before?" Henn poured himself another cup of coffee.

"You have that prosecutor's edge."

"Good, good. I'll get you all I can."

"I'd like to see anything else you might have. You know, Attorney Henn, to examine it from my perspective." Rook took a couple of the lawyer's business cards for show. "You hear of any lawyers making claims?"

"If they haven't, they will. There's signs all up and down the highway, television commercials, whatever. I don't do that." Henn drank the coffee down. "I believe in establishing relationships. That's what brings clients. You need anything else, just ask."

"Who's your police chief?" Lucas asked.

"Bill Jarmaluck. Been the Chief of Police for almost fifteen years. County Sheriff before that. Fred Blum's County Sheriff now. Blum and Jarmaluck, they don't like each other one bit. Something to do with the Beck case. Most unbelievable case in my years at the bar."

"Is that a fact?"

"Unbelievable. You just wouldn't believe it…"

Rook got up. "Call over to Chief Jarmaluck for me, will ya Peter? You know, your experience with the prosecutor's office. Tell him I'm on my way over to pay my respects and that I work for Mrs. Politte."

"Will do. Will do."

"Thanks for the coffee, counselor. It was mighty good." Rook went out the creaky door and over to meet the police.

❦   ❦   ❦

Webster Clark looked at his steel-cased watch. He could get everything done before the traffic strangled the streets. Getting across town was impossible, and it now was a thriving cottage industry writing up all the cars that got stuck partly in the intersection. He stayed on the lower West side and found a meter on Eighth Avenue. A double-decker bus went by with tourists freezing in the wind as they leered at hippies and homosexuals.

Clark went over to Damer's and had some miso soup.

"Got a sale on C-1000," Damer said. "With and without bioflavonoids."

"I'm good."

"Knew a guy stayed on that macrobiotic diet for a year. Nothing but brown rice and miso soup. They did another x-ray, he came up clean as a baby."

Clark nodded.

"Got scurvy through. He surely did. George Osawa wouldn't have lasted a week in all this pollution."

Web sipped his soup. "I just like the way it tastes."

A short girl in an orange coat with rhinestone buttons came in. She had on platform shoes with candy striped heels.

"You got raw milk?" she asked.

"Can't sell that no more, missy," the proprietor told her. "Got certified organic goat's milk and a sale on soy milk. And not that stuff they sell in the supermarket. This is cold-pressed."

Damer's two little dogs came running out from the back. "Alphonse! Gastone! You get back."

The girl in the orange coat hid behind Webster Clark.

"They won't bite," the storekeeper said as his dogs went barking at the girl's shoes.

She kicked at them, and the white dog went yipping across the room.

"You kicked my dog," said Damer. "You evil crazy thing. Must be all filled with heavy metals. Bet your mouth's full of mercury fillings." He picked Alphonse up. "You get on out of here and don't come back until you been chelated a good bit."

"Well, fuck all four of you then," she said. "My name's Pure Magic and you all can go fuck yourselves." The girl in the orange coat went back outside, her coat twinkling.

Webster Clark had a fresh-made celery and apple juice and bought a bottle of lycopene. Then he went over to the St. Claire. Mrs. Grayboyes had her arms full of shopping, and that was enough to get him easily by the desk. He rode the elevator up to the fourth floor, then took the steps the rest of the way up to Rook's.

There were impediments, but Clark got into the apartment without detection. He had allotted a half hour to learn everything about Lucas Rook. He checked the medicine cabinet, refrigerator, closets, and drawers. The gun safe contained two .45's, a .38 with a two-inch barrel, and a throwdown piece. The ammunition was Black Talon, glaser, and some msc's.

The refrigerator held two cans of tuna fish, some genoa salami, and a half-dozen eggs. Rook kept a can of coffee in the fridge, and Web checked it for another gun. That was still happening since *The Rockford Files*.

He moved the odd collection of books, Joseph Wambaugh and Joseph Conrad, Masad Ayoob, and Beryl Markham. A stack of *Shotgun News*. A book of love poems by Jack Palance with an inscription from "Cat."

Web Clark went into the bedroom. A rolled towel on the bed. Rook's shoes were worn unevenly. Two suits, two sport coats, a lined raincoat. A cane that fired a .44. Naughty, naughty. In the bureau drawer were some yellowed clippings. Kirk Rook murdered. The picture on the mantelpiece. A letter from Catherine Wren, postmarked Princeton.

Clark made himself a cup of tea and milk and sipped it in the first dark room. A woman singing outside. He went to watch her, beautiful, angular, blind. She tended to her flowers, stroking their leaves, talking to them, turning away to exhale her cigarette smoke.

It was time to go. He washed the teacup and left. He had two more stops to make. Web had promised Virginia he'd bring her a piece of New York cheesecake. He went in the corner deli. The counterman left the twin towers of corned beef he had sliced and cut a piece of the rich, white cake.

"Make it two," Clark said. He went to feed the meter and eat his piece of dessert. Then he walked around the block to the garage. The back door was easy. He thought about killing the dog, but it went back to sleep. Then he took the hammer from his coat and broke Sid Rosen's head.

CHAPTER 10

Lucas put his weapon in the trunk of his rental before he went in to pay his respects to the locals. He kept his NYPD shield in his right pocket, his PI identification in his left.

The Oneonta Police Department shared the Public Safety Building with the Fire Department and the local court. There were piles of salt and sand and trucks off to the left. The cruisers and a police van were to the right. The sign outside said, "The Life You Save Might Be Your Own." The directory in the lobby told him where the chief was.

The deputy, whose name was Heavens, sat behind plexiglass.

"I'd like to see Chief Jarmaluck."

Deputy Richard Heavens adjusted the chin strap of his hat. "You got an appointment?"

"Just paying my respects."

"You got to make an appointment for such as that."

Rook showed his gold shield.

Heavens had a dip of smokeless under his front lip and sucked on it. "You got any other proof of identity?"

After thoroughly examining Rook's credentials, he called into the chief's secretary and told Lucas he'd have to return in an hour.

Rook drove back into town. The Traveler's coffee shop served breakfast and lunch. Dinner on Sunday afternoons and Wednesday, which was probably bingo night.

The waitress should not have been wearing a short skirt. "Grilled sticky bun is good, so is the special," she said.

"Now what might that be?"

She looked at the back of her order pad. "Three eggs, any style, toast, ham steak with a pineapple slice. Coffee's fresh."

Lucas got the sticky bun and coffee and little else except that the people from the Bottle House "were a different crowd" and ate "up the other end." The waitress' sister-in-law knew one of the people that died and that was a shame, but "the Lord works in mysterious ways. Praise the Lord."

Lucas read in the paper about a new mall coming up and that the community college was building a new gym. A man with a turkey neck watched him from under his John Deere hat. Rook let that go and went back up to the police department to check in.

This time a female officer named Olson sat behind the glass. She had a cigarette burning on the counter next to her. "Can I help you?" she asked.

"I have an appointment with Chief Jarmaluck."

She called into the back and then was told that there was no such appointment.

"I have an appointment with Chief Jarmaluck. The name is Rook."

Officer Olson buzzed the Chief's office again. "I'm sorry," she said. "You do have a 10:30 appointment. It is only 10:15. That's what I checked on. The Chief's in a conference."

"Will he be rescheduling this appointment?"

"I won't know until he's free."

Rook sat down on one of the gray chairs bolted to the floor. There was an old *Sports Illustrated*. He checked his watch, stretched his leg and started the article on the Japanese wide receiver playing in the NFL.

In another ten minutes, Officer Olson invited him back. She had great tits and another cigarette burning.

Rook followed her. The Chief was talking on the phone with his back turned. Olson held Rook at the entrance to the office. The room was filled with plaques, hats, and tee-shirts from local organizations and other PD's.

The Chief turned and smiled. He had enough braid and medals on his uniform to be the Joint Chief of Staff, and thick glasses.

"Nice ride up from the City?" he said. "Me and the wife go down there at Christmas time to see the tree at Rockefeller Center."

Lucas knew they had used the extra time to run his car and name. "Nice town you have here, Oneonta."

"We like to think so. Attorney Henn said you're working for Mrs. Politte. That's fine with me, though I don't know what for." He moved around one of the awards on his desk. "Why don't you tell me about it?"

"It's a matter of insurance, Chief. She needs risk management evaluation after the deaths at the plant. The insurance company wants to know everything's under control."

"Got to keep the plant running. That's important." He adjusted his glasses and rang a little fire bell with his finger. "I appreciate your stopping in. You need anything, you just call. But two things, Mr. Rook."

Lucas let him go on.

"Don't be flashing your gold shield because of your being an ex-cop. I checked. And second, don't be unholstering your weapon either, which I assume you got a permit for." The Chief stood up. "You get anything, you bring it to me. Being a cowboy isn't going to get you anywheres you'll want to be."

They shook hands. Jarmaluck's grip was strong.

Donna Olson came in and brought Rook back out. "You staying long?" she asked.

"I don't think so," he answered.

"Have a nice day," she said as she lit up another Kool.

Rook backed his Crown Vic out of its slot and drove over to *The Daily*. It was a small town newspaper, but the masthead made it look like it had a decent staff. Editor-in-chief, associate editors for the various features, a separate department for advertising, and one for circulation. There were no reporters in, which meant they used part-timers and stringers. The associate editor's name was Rudnicki, an angular man with faded blonde hair. He wore a sport coat without a tie.

"How can I help you, Mr. Rook?"

"I'm working for the insurance company for the Bottle House. About the deaths they had over there."

Rudnicki reached for a cigarette from the pack inside his desk. He lit up, turning to exhale the smoke behind him. "Well, I'd say you were in law enforcement, certainly from New York City, your accent is a dead giveaway, and from your gait, I'd say you're on disability. How am I doing?"

"Fairly well. I'm hoping you could be giving me some information or I could go over to your library and get it. I do that, I get anything of interest for you, I give it to the local TV station instead."

The newspaper man snubbed the cigarette out like he was making art. "Fair enough. What do you want to know?"

Rudnicki filled Rook in on the basic business climate and the community. He knew about the deaths of the plant's employees, but only because of the obits. He gave an advertising rate card and wished Lucas good luck.

Rook thanked him and left. He waited the count of ten, then

opened the door without knocking. Rudnicki was on the phone with Chief Jarmaluck.

Lucas drove over to Mrs. Politte's factory. Halfway there he saw a black truck following him. It slowed and speeded up when he did. Rook jumped the red light and did a U-turn until he was alongside. It was his new friend, "Turkey Neck." There was a sticker on the rear window of a tree whose branches spelled "Liberty."

"Morning," Rook said.

The man tried to pull his John Deere hat down.

"I'm going over to the Bottle House a mile or so ahead. You want, I'll drive nice and slow so you don't lose me."

Turkey Neck gave him the finger, then slowly pulled away.

※　　※　　※

Webster Clark needed to rest when he got to the Holiday Inn on Western Avenue. It was only a little more than an hour from Oneonta, but his cancer pain and the meds were getting to him. He wondered whether somehow he had decided to base in Albany rather than closer in because there was a good hospital there. He hoped not.

Web ran the plates on the pick-up truck before he got into bed. If Virginia was with him, they would ride over to Saratoga Springs and stop at Moon's Lake where the brochure said the first potato chips were made, or to the Cambridge Hotel where they first served pie-a-la-mode. Now he slept alone In his dream, they were sitting on their porch that curved into the trees, but there were arc lights overhead and they wore jungle clothes. The smell of orange rain was in the air, Agent Orange rain.

CHAPTER 11

Billy Gamon expected his dinner to be ready when he came home from the Bottle House, and he didn't hesitate to let his wife know about it. "Pean, I don't smell nothing cooking." He untied his steel-tips and left them on the newspaper she had spread inside the front door. "I don't smell nothing cooking," he said again.

Peanut Gamon pushed her hair away from her face and lit another cigarette as she stirred the black skillet. "Sound like you're getting a cold, Bill. I'll put some hots in the casserole."

He took one of her smokes. "Where's young Billy, Pean? He's supposed to be here when I get home."

"You're supposed to not be leaving yours in the truck and smoking all mine up. Young Billy, he's next door playing with their new dog."

Billy Gamon's face reddened. "You know I don't like that, Pean. You know that's not right, his being there."

She slid over to the fridge and popped him open a beer. "Bill, he ain't going to be catching nothing, and their boy's his age. Besides, they called from work for me to come in."

He grabbed her by the arm and took her over to the drugstore calendar that hung on the basement door. "You know I got a meeting tonight. You know that from me telling you and from looking at the calendar."

Peanut pulled away and rubbed her arm. "That's going to leave a mark, Bill. That's not right. Now why don't you change your socks and sit down for the casserole. Daddy told me he was coming by to pick you up."

He went into the front room and sat down on the bed. He hated that them Portuguese had moved next door, especially since they had new siding which he had hoped to put up himself, but enough OT hadn't come through.

There was an unopened pack of Winstons in his top drawer where he kept his pistol and he lit up another cigarette, using the beer can as an ashtray. "It's all screwed up," he said out loud, but there was nobody to hear him. Outside the window he could see a flash of Little Billy go by and the black-haired boy from next door, who was bigger than him by a head. The dog tied up outside barked and barked.

Pean kept Billy's supper warm until he came in to eat and poured them each a beer. She picked the pearl onions from her plate and spooned them over to Bill. "They asked me about picking up either Saturday mornings or Sundays, the holidays coming up."

"Sundays ain't right."

"I just got more orders to make up is all, Bill."

Bill shook his head and ate in silence. Then he got up to get another beer. "Convenience store up near the interstate got took over by some Arabs," he said. He rubbed the mark branded on his arm.

Pean got up. She shuffled a little when she walked. "I got to go to work. Be back right after eight. I'll get Billy on the way." She tried a smile. "Told them Portuguese not to give him no octopus to eat."

"Screwed up," Gamon said and went back to their room.

She took two cigarettes from her pack and left them on the nightstand. "Daddy said he's coming to pick you up."

Billy exhaled streams of smoke through his nose.

"May I have the keys please, Bill? I can't be walking over to the store."

He pointed to the bureau.

The top drawer was open and Peanut saw his pistol there. "You getting that lock box you promised?"

"Thought Santy Claus would've brought it." He snubbed his smoke. "Young Billy knows better anyways."

She took back one of the cigarettes and lit it as she went out to work.

At a little after six, Cal Treaster drove up and honked the horn. He adjusted his John Deere hat as his son-in-law got in the station wagon.

"See you got the back cleaned out, Cal. You expecting somebody?"

"Aluminum next door looks good," he said. "Cold's not good for Peanut, never was." Treaster spun up a spray of gravel as he backed out of the driveway. "They putting part-timers on over at Cooperstown if you can stand what the niggers and the spics done to baseball. Me, been working that second job and the dye plant for nine years now."

Cal Treaster drove on for the next twenty minutes without saying another word. The radio didn't work, and Bill Gamon knew better than to say anything else.

They parked in the back of Heinsel's Lumber. As they got out of the station wagon, Cal and Billy Gamon rolled up their sleeves so all could see the half-moon branded on their arms.

❦ ❦ ❦

The Bottle House was a three-story brick building that had been painted gray a long time ago. It was across a one-way street from the new Clarion Motor Hotel on the way out of Oneonta. There was screening over the windows and a giant concrete milk bottle out front.

The guard leaned out of the security booth as Rook pulled up. He was an old man with a fried egg sandwich in his hand.

"I've got an appointment with Ms. Charney."

"Who's she?"

"She's the Director of Human Resources."

"You sure of that?"

Lucas opened his window some more. "I'm sure."

"You got I.D.? You got to show your driver's license."

"I got a driver's license. Seems to me your egg sandwich going to get cold."

"Like it cold. You pull over up against the building there. Make sure to stay within them lines."

"Will do, Chief." Lucas pulled over and parked in the open space furthest from the steps.

There was a security desk just inside the door with a sign-in book. Rook was putting on his badge when the guard walked up. He looked a lot like the one at the gate.

"I'm here to see Ms. Charney," Rook told him.

"Don't know her. You got ID? Told you out at the gate you got to show ID."

Lucas showed his driver's license. "Now you know her?"

"Ms. Charney, right, Human Resources. I take my job serious. You got an appointment, you go right up them stairs, turn right, then left. Don't be making two rights 'cause then you got to be wearing a hard hat."

The stairwell smelled strong from cigarette smoke, and the iron steps were littered with butts. As Rook started up, he saw a shadow on the wall and the fire door open and close. He followed the directions and found himself at a freshly painted door with the words "Director of Human Resources" being stenciled on.

The painter looked over his shoulder. "Finishing up," he said. "Now watch that paint. Put a sign up says 'Wet Paint,' but that'd be wet too."

There was a small outer office inside. On the walls were a calendar from the Soccer Hall of Fame, a poster of a cat hanging from a branch, and a changeable sign that read "306 days without an accident." The receptionist was a large woman with a bad auburn dye-job. The steel nameplate on her desk said, "Martha Brookhouser."

"I have an appointment with Ms. Charney."

She scrolled up on her computer. "And you would be Mr. Nuke?"

"Rook, Martha."

"Of course it is." She leaned closer to the screen. "Although I would have pronounced it 'Ruke.' And please call me Ms. Brookhouser. If you'll just take a seat, I'll let her know."

There were industrial magazines, a copy of the newspaper and an old *Boy's Life* addressed to Everett Brookhouser. Lucas waited for almost a half hour before Martha had anything to say. "Sorry for the delay, Mr. Rook. If you want, there's a coffee machine down the hall."

Lucas Rook got up and took the opportunity to look around. There were two offices next door. The closest one had nothing on the door. The furthest said "Quality Control." The coffee machine was at the other end of the hall, just beyond a broad yellow line marked "Hard Hat Area."

Two men with dust masks hanging down were talking about openings at the Corning Plant. They were wearing long-sleeve shirts and sweating heavily.

"Takes only exact change. No matter what it says," the big one said.

The other one had a lazy eye that seemed to be looking towards the right. "Thirty-five cents. Quarter and a dime. That's exact change. Won't take two nickels."

Rook fished for the change. "As long as it's hot."

Big Earl Joost edged in front of the coffee machine. "Got to have a hard hat you cross that yellow line."

Rook gave him his mean cop look. "I'm a nasty man when I don't have my coffee."

"You a Yankees fan, Mr. Nasty Man?"

Rook spread his stance a bit. "Right now I'm a man who needs his coffee."

Earl Joost stepped away as Edna Charney came down the hall. With her hard hat she was as big as most men. She had a growth the size of a peanut on her jaw. "Boys," she acknowledged. "And you must be Mr. Rook? Coffee's better in my office, and this is a hard hat area."

They walked back down the hall. "Boys here are pretty sensitive since the Yankees moved their farm team from here down to Staten Island. Particularly Earl, who played first base in high school, although they moved a good ten years after his playing days."

"Sorry reason to break your streak, Ms. Charney."

"And what streak would that be?"

Lucas pointed to the 306 sign. Edna smiled. "Two coffees, Martha, please." They went inside her office. There were diplomas on the wall from State University of New York and Hardwick College and a certificate from the Society of Human Resource Managers. The only picture was one of her standing in front of a red door.

"The insurance carrier sent you? I have our risk management well under control."

"There's deaths, it's something that's got to be looked at."

Martha brought the coffee in with Cremora and Sweet N' Low on the tray. Both of them took it black. Rook went on, "Especially with the possibility of workplace violence."

She put her cup down, then wiped a drop of coffee that had spilled. "There's no workplace violence here in my plant. I have a strong policy against that. And we have training and referral to psych services over at Fox Hospital should anybody begin to act out.

"The deaths? There's nothing suspicious about them, Mr. Rook. People get sick and die. The Board of Health's been over here. No e-coli, listeria, or any of that. People always talking about that since what happened in Pennsylvania in those meat packing plants." She reached into the middle drawer of her desk. "Here are the personnel files of those who died. No problems to speak of, although the col-ored girl had a habit of misusing her leave." She poured herself an-other half cup of coffee. "You can review the files. My Policies and Procedures are in our Employee Handbook. I've set up a desk for you next door. If you want to interview any of the employees, advise me first. Also, our union agreement requires that I tell the shop steward."

"I appreciate that. By the way, Ms. Charney, tell me about the big cement bottle out front."

"Used to be we produced more milk around here than anywhere else, they say. And hand-rolled cigars. But we do just fine without them."

Rook stood up. "I'll be grabbing something to eat across the street when I'm done with those files and anybody you've suspended or terminated in the last couple years. Then I'd like to take a look at your plant. The insurance carrier's idea really. I'd just as soon get back to Manhattan."

"So you'll be staying over?"

"At the Clarion. It looks brand new."

Edna Charney smiled and said goodbye without shaking hands.

CHAPTER 12

Rook remembered the first time he sat down with somebody's jacket. Jim McCullagh was looking over his shoulder and pointing at things in the file. "You see this. You see that. He got no high school diploma, no GED, no service, and he's selling insurance. What does that tell you about the guy?" He threw down another file. "See this mutt, he can't keep away from chicks with ponytails or boosting Corvettes. No way he doesn't get popped again before New Year's," McCullagh said.

Lucas Rook looked at the files on Jackie Moore and Arnetta Holmes like he had all the thousands of files he had seen at the NYPD and since he went private. Employment files were set up differently because of the rules and regulations, the medicals separate so there was no possibility of health-related discrimination and the like. But work files told a good story, because they had criminal record and background checks and lots of personal information.

Jackie Moore was twenty-six, married to Marie and taking three deductions on his income tax. He had used Family Medical Leave when their daughter was born. There were three different addresses since he started at the Bottle House. The person to call in case of emergency was his father, Jack Moore, who also worked at the plant. There was a wage attachment for support for a son, John Joseph Moore, III. His drug screens had never come up hot, and his criminal records abstract was clean except for a disorderly and public intox at Lake George. Jackie Moore, born John Joseph Moore, Jr., had received the usual step-promotions, and his widow had collected the factory funeral benefit of four hundred dollars.

Lucas started to take notes on the Arnetta Holmes file when Martha Brookhouser came in without knocking. "Ms. Charney said you wanted to see more files." She handed over a few folders. "Ms. Charney also said if you desire copies of anything, I am to do it and only after I check with her first."

"She said all that, did she? Well tell Ms. Charney that I appreciate it, but now with all this work, there's no way you and I can have lunch together." Martha Brookhouser left without a word.

Arnetta Holmes' file had a little more meat to it, as did Arnetta herself. She was five feet six and weighed one hundred and eighty-five pounds. She was not married although she had two children. Her leave records showed time-off to care for a grandson, DeVille Williams, and a great granddaughter, Jaleesa Clayton. Somewhere along the line Arnetta still had found time to graduate from Emmons High School and take two courses at the Community College. The subject did pull a DUI on her twenty-first birthday and had a Protection from Abuse Complaint filed against her by a Darnell Payton. At work, she used her leave as fast as she earned it and had no carry-over. Despite this, she was twice elected as a union rep and for six months was alternate steward. Her funeral benefits had not yet been paid, but had been claimed by both her sister and a Milton Harper, who described himself as Ms. Holmes' common-law husband.

The new file material brought in by Martha was scant. One

termination, one voluntary suspension to avoid, and six instances of serious violations, including two by Jack Curran for fighting.

So many people to see, places to go. It made Lucas Rook think about a couple of beers. Perhaps he could share a pitcher with Big Earl and his cross-eyed sidekick.

It was lunchtime for the shift. Lucas waited until the wave of them went across the side street to The Bumper, a converted rail shed. Rook wondered whether there were pool tables inside or it got its name from Nattie Bumpo, the local folk hero created by the omnipresent local author, James Fenimore Cooper.

There must have been a hundred sweating men packed into the airless place that should have held less than half that much. Pushing their way towards the bar, coming back, both hands filled with mugs and bottles. A few of them were standing at the bar, like Big Earl, and down the other end was a huge black man with a shaved head. They looked like they weren't going anywhere. Turkey Neck in his John Deere hat was next to Earl, talking over his shoulder to a group of men.

"Draught and a bump," a man in a paper hat called out as he reached the bar.

Another with a stump for a hand asked for a boilermaker for himself and a second one for his sickly child. Three girls sat at a table in the back, drinking as good as any men.

"To Arnetta Holmes," said one girl with her hair still in a net.

One drank with both hands, and the short girl with the curly hair sat with her head down and her empty glass held high.

Half the house had seen Rook standing off to the side, as did Georgie White, the bartender, who was trying to keep up with the drinking and the time running down. Thirty minutes was all they had, less two minutes over and three to get back.

"You know him?" Georgie asked. "Standing over there like he's some spy or something?"

"I do not," Holdsworth said. "Keep pouring."

"Big Earl says he's the insurance man," Lazy Eye said.

"I'll ask him when you're done," the barkeep said.

The shop steward tapped the bottom of his glass on the bar. So did Big Earl. Georgie poured a draft and slid it down the bar. By the time it arrived, he had poured Earl's cold one and the bump.

"Looks like a cop," Bill Gamon said. "A lot of them insurance men were cops."

The bartender gave Lucas Rook a hard stare, and Jack Moore came in. He walked slowly, like he was pulling a sled of rocks. Everyone let him pass.

Georgie White poured him a Seagrams and water. Cal Treaster nodded, his turkey neck wattling back and forth. The black man said something and put his drink down.

"You coming back to work, Jack?" the bartender asked.

Jack Moore drank his first drink and sipped the next. "Dunno" is all he said.

"Countdown," Georgie called.

"Three minutes," Big Earl confirmed.

The ones in the rear came forward and everybody got all they could before they started back, slapping money on the bar and calling it out for Georgie to hear.

The black man walked slow. "Shop steward got its rank and privileges," he said out loud.

There were only three men left and one drunk girl. She wanted to give blowjobs, but there were no takers. "Go on home, Elaine," White said, wiping down the bar. "It ain't right you being here like that."

Jack Moore sat down when she got up. He slid the ashtrays and the empties over to the side so he could enjoy his drink. Lucas Rook sat down at the table. "I'm sorry about your loss," he said. "I'm from the insurance company for the plant."

"Marie, she's got the funeral money."

Rook sipped his beer. "There's other money might be coming.

Family uses a lawyer, the blood suckers get their cut."

"Dead is dead."

"Your son left two kids, and my company might be prepared to write a check."

"Dead's still dead, compo or whatever included." Jack Moore looked into the bottom of his glass. "Maybe we got nothing to talk about. Maybe we already talked to a lawyer, there's plenty of them up the road."

Lucas sipped his beer. "I don't have all I need. Ms. Charney's not too helpful."

"Wouldn't figure she'd be unless you got a young wife she wants. Turned that secretary of hers into a regular pussy sucking maniac." He held up his right hand for another drink. "Four's my limit. Me, I don't know how he died. He got sick, he died. Only thing good about it all, his mother passed last Christmas. She'd have killed herself for sure she been around to see this."

"I need something to rule out the things we don't insure, Jack. Was he sick before? Did he have a family doctor?"

"Me nor him never been sick." Another Seagrams came. "You're frankly wearing me out, Mister. County Health came in. Said Jackie got some stomach thing went bad."

"Arnetta Holmes, Jack? You know her?"

"You were wearing me out, Mister, and now you're pissing me off. I'd say we're done here."

"I guess we are, Jack. I guess we are." Rook left a couple of bucks on the sticky table. He'd go across to the Clarion and grab some lunch. Then he'd look at the termination files and check into the Holiday Inn. When Turkey Neck saw him start to leave the table, he left the doorway and went around to the back where he parked his truck.

The décor in the Clarion's "The Leatherstocking Room" reminded Rook of early James Fenimore Cooper and late cocktail lounge.

"Sounds like an S & M joint," Rook said to the waitress.

She stroked her hair. "Our special today is tenderloin tips over rice and a visit to the salad bar."

"And the meatloaf, how's that?"

"That's our special too."

"What do you suggest, Maureen?"

She looked surprised he knew her name. He pointed to the name-plate on her black uniform.

"They're all good. The company makes the airline food makes it."

Lucas put the menu down. "Club sandwich will be good, Maureen. Mayo on the side. Nice place here. Nice town. Shame I had to come up here for the funeral, and late at that."

She went away and came back with a cup of coffee. "I know," was all she said.

A fat girl brought the check. Rook left a big tip even though the club sandwich tasted like airline food. "Tell Maureen I said thanks. She doing dinner too?"

"She only does breakfasts and lunches. You know, the kids and all."

Lucas smiled and put two dollars in her chubby hand. "Thank you too," he told her with a smile.

Rook went back to the factory. The room he had used before was locked. He went next door to Human Resources. Ms. Brookhouser's desk was empty and the door to the inner office was closed. He sat down and read the *Daily* again. The obituaries listed the same funeral home, except for one in Albany and one in Cooperstown. He'd pay a visit when he was done at the factory.

Lucas was starting an old *National Geographic* when he heard the two coming down the hall. Both Ms. Charney and her secretary had on New York Jets jogging suits.

"A pleasant lunch, Mr. Rook?" The HR director patted herself with a towel.

"The Clarion's famous for their club sandwiches. I can see why."

"Can I help you?" Ms. Brookhouser asked.

"I'd like to see all the rest of the disciplinary action files, voluntary separations to avoid terminations and disciplinary actions."

"Of course you would. Ms. Brookhouser will provide those shortly." Ms. Charney went into her office to change.

"Next door is locked," Rook told the receptionist.

"Of course it is." Martha took a key from the middle drawer. "Just let me freshen up. I'll have you that paperwork in a jiffy."

"Two jiffies will be fine. And don't forget the videotape of your employee theft."

"I don't know anything about such a tape."

In another twenty minutes she came back with the personnel folders. There was a line of talcum powder on her neck.

"How about those Jets?" he said.

Ms. Brookhouser looked at him for a minute. "I'm not much of a sports fan. And Ms. Charney said the tape was sent to the Unemployment Compensation Board. We do oppose unwarranted applications here."

"Joe Namath wore panty-hose for his knees," Lucas said, but she left without a comment.

There was a stack of files going back four years. Most suspensions were for abusing time, Louis Fleck being the greatest offender. He also got two days off for urinating on the packing floor. There were three suspensions for fighting, two given out to Jack Curran and one to Art Irwin. Irwin's file indicated that he died in a hunting accident six months ago.

Two of the files were involuntary separations. Rudy Knoll had five years at the Bottle House when he was terminated for stealing. Lucas copied down the address and phone number. The other termination was the former head of quality control, Frank Carillo, for sexual harassment. Carillo had a Master of Science degree in chemistry from San Diego State. Divorced, one dependent, which could have been himself, his ex or a kid.

Carillo's file contained the complaint by a Sherry Reiner, who alleged quid pro quo harassment. "Even after I told him that I was not interested, he persisted in saying that if I did him, he would see that I got all the overtime I could handle." There was an internal investigative report signed by Ms. Charney. No response had been submitted by the alleged harasser.

A separate folder in Carillo's file detailed his application for Unemployment Compensation. It also contained a strong memo from Edna Charney opposing the company's decision not to appeal his award of unemployment, which had been granted because Ms. Reiner did not testify. Rook copied down the most recent address for Frank Carillo.

Sitting in that office was getting to be too much like desk duty. Lucas Rook drove out to Jackie Moore's place. Brent Road was a turning, narrow street so that halfway in, the cars parked on the south side of the street made it possible to get down the block without going up on the sidewalk. An old man sat on a kitchen chair at the turn of the bend.

"C'mon up and hit me, you yellow son of a bitch," he yelled as the cars came by. Once he tried to spit in the driver's side window.

"What's this all about?" Lucas asked the old man.

"You, you yellow son of a bitch!"

"Is that right, partner? Thought I could count on you. Thought you were holding down the fort."

The old man lungered up another spit.

"Going to have to reassign this vital position, you keep acting like that. Now you just hold the fort until the real big ones come on by. You'll know them when you see them."

Jackie Moore's house was up two steps to a landing and three steps after that. The doorbell didn't work. He knocked twice. No one answered. Lucas went next door.

A young girl with a baby in her arms answered. "Marie's gone to the lady next door on the other side. The house with the blue trim. I got to whisper or my own one here going to wake up, and then it's no small job to get him back to sleep. He's so bad he'll be waking up at the dropping of a pin." She tried a little pout.

"You know Jackie and Marie?" Rook said.

Her baby started to stir. "Now let me just get him down before my stories come on."

Rook decided to let it go. Come back after Marie got the word from her father-in-law that there might be an insurance check around. He looked at his watch. It would be stretching it to go by Arnetta Holmes'. He'd get that billing in tomorrow.

CHAPTER 13

It was right after break-time of the second shift when Dirty Louis Fleck fell down dead on the Bottle House packing floor. Danny-boy went over and gave him a shove.

"You pounding too many of them seven-ounce ponies, Dirty Lou. Too many of them fine green bottles of amber suds," said Danny-boy.

"Amber's a fine word," said Pearl, fluffing up her hair. She turned to the big man curled up. "Now get on up, Lou, before somebody comes along."

When they saw that Dirty Lou wasn't getting up at all, they called the nurse. Big Earl called the safety officer.

Nurse Margaret Clymer came up slowly in her white shoes, breathing hard. They were glad to see her, even though she only ever gave out the little packs of Tylenol and sometimes Motrin when the girls were on their curse. She held her fingers to her face. "Louis Fleck, you drunk again?"

"He's dead, I think," said Pearl, fluffing her hair again.

Nurse Clymer walked over close in her big white shoes. Her stance told all that there was no way she could reach the corpse to take the vital signs. The safety officer, whose name was Lee, got Dirty Lou up a bit so she could feel his pulse.

"He's dead," she said. "I'm sure of that."

The steward, who was earning some overtime, walked in slowly. "Maybe he's just in a stupor."

"He's dead, Mr. Wright. I'm sure of that," Nurse Clymer said again.

"You could use my compact mirror to check his breath," called Pearl.

"The handbook says we're to call Ms. Charney," said Lazy Eye.

"You do that, Duffy," said Steward Wright. "Me, I'd rather call in the state police than be calling Edna Charney at her home. Nurse Clymer says he's dead, that's good enough for me." He stepped back a step and turned so that he was facing them all. "This union takes care of its own," he said.

Nurse Clymer felt faint. Back in her office she took a pill and gave a sigh. She called Edna Charney. The phone rang six times before she picked it up.

"I'm there in life and in death," said the Director of Human Resources to the nurse and then to Ms. Brookhouser before she lay her back down.

When she was done, Ms. Charney washed herself and drove in to the Bottle House in her 4x4. Louis Fleck had been an obese drunk who used booze and cigarettes like they were fresh air. Now he was a pile of dead flesh generating a pile of paperwork.

It was her job to see that all the benefits were paid. She'd call Mrs. Fleck after confirming that Lou had in fact, expired. Betty Fleck was flighty and half a drunk herself, so she'd have to write up the benefits, bring a copy and mail her one.

Everyone at the plant would be told again about the grief counselor down at the hospital and Candy Fleck, his niece, the slut, would be allowed one day bereavement leave. The health department would have to be out again to check that it was no industrial accident or violent act and that it didn't meet the profile on the list of Legionnaire's, Listeria, West Nile, TB or AIDS.

Edna Charney shook her head. What would the Health Department find except that dead Louis Edward Fleck was a smelly, drunken pig? In any case, she would have to write up what Nurse Clymer and the safety officer saw and all about the benefits. Her report would be comprehensive and accurate.

By the time the Director of Human Resources arrived at the Bottle House, Dirty Lou was lying in the nurse's room. Margaret Clymer had protested that there was only one bed and somebody may have to lay down because they felt faint or had a bad headache or bad cramps and who was going to clean up because of the way he was all soiled and such.

Ms. Charney witnessed that Louis Fleck had died, then went to her office to make the calls. The application for employment said to call his wife in case of emergency. Maybe the form should say who to call when I puke myself for the very last time. She called Betty Fleck and told her matter-of-factly.

"Is there somebody else I should call, Mrs. Fleck?"

"Excuse me?"

"Is there somebody I should call?" said Edna Charney.

"I was lying down."

"About your husband, Mrs. Fleck. Louis died at work tonight. I told you that."

"He won't be coming home?"

"He's dead, Mrs. Fleck."

"He won't be coming home. My Louis is not coming home," Betty Fleck said twice.

Edna Charney hung up. It was the shift's lunch break. Time for the sweating herd to run across the road and come back smashed.

An extra excuse tonight. "Here's to my best friend, Lou."

She checked her pocket watch. She'd look at Fleck's benefits, then do a walk-through of the plant before she went home. Shipping and Receiving was on the first floor behind the offices and behind that, the loading dock. There were two trucks up against the plant.

Everybody was at their posts in the Loose Room. The machines started up again on the packing floor. The mixing room was filled with workers dressed like they were from outer space. Ken Holdsworth ran by, his mask not up and only one shoe covered like it should be.

"Where to, Kenny? Surprised to see me on this shift?"

He didn't stop.

"I'm writing you up," she called.

"That's not right," dared someone else. "His wife just called. Their kid is real sick."

❧   ❧   ❧

When the long haul truck was loaded up, Ray Enfield came back, the big buckle on his belt shining bright and his shitkickers wiped clean. He adjusted his fine black Stetson. "Heading out," he said.

"Driving straight through?" the checker from the Bottle House asked.

"It's where the money is if my kidneys don't bounce out first. Buy myself a set of gold teeth with a diamond stud in every one."

Bobby Paul laughed and shook his head at the thought of the trucker all niggered-up.

Ray Enfield climbed up in his rig. "Adios amigos," he said. He drove hard. Sometimes it was like he was in a cell, being awake in the dark, but he had settled on a way of doing things. Running in the night meant less fuel, because he could ride with the AC off, and there were things he liked, the night air going by and the owls calling.

The truckstop served good food and the rooms were clean. Ray spread the packs of sugar out and ordered himself a stack with eggs and ham. The coffee was hot.

Miss Lucy watched him go at the cakes and ham and eggs. "I bet you could eat an elephant!" she said.

He lit himself a smoke. "Wished I had a cat," was all he said.

The strip of motel rooms with orange doors was off to the left. A cleaning cart with soap and towels stood in front of number six as the rain came down.

Nancy Lynne with her new teeth walked by, asking if he needed help to get to sleep. Ray waved her off and went inside. He sat on the bed and poured himself some gin.

Tomorrow he'd make his first drop. There'd be someone there to unload and pack the cartons of diet bars back in tight as he headed off again. The final drop was New York City. Then back again. He fell asleep dreaming of the cat.

C H A P T E R

There was another hour before check-in time at the Holiday Inn. After he returned the files, Lucas Rook went back to the oasis of the coffee machine, always a fertile spot. Maybe he'd run into Big Earl again, a bad guy with bad stuff coming off of him.

Earl wasn't there, but Lazy Eye was, along with the black man he had seen at the bar. "You the insurance man. My name's Wright. I'm the shop steward, and you supposed to be wearing a hard hat across this yellow line." He sipped the coffee Lazy Eye Duffy handed him. "Sometimes you can't win for losing."

"How's that?" Rook said.

"You going to have to be opening up that checkbook again. Another one of my members just died. Louis Fleck dropped dead right here at work. Got to be compo, no matter what you say."

Lazy Eye waited for another two cups to fill up and put them in the small cardboard box he carried.

"Where's your big, ugly friend?" Lucas asked him.

"Don't be stirring things up in my house," the steward said.

"Seems it's Mrs. Politte's house, not yours."

"Manner of speaking, that's true." Wright looked at his watch and then at Lazy Eye. "You stretching breaktime. Get on back."

Duffy took his box of coffees and left, looking both ways as he did.

"Coffee's bad," Rook said.

"Seems you'd be used to that."

Lucas took another sip. "Why's that?"

"I know a cop when I see one," Wright said.

"Used to be. You been jammed up before?"

Wright smiled, but his eyes said something else. "I love that patois, 'jammed up.' Me, no, I haven't been jammed up, but I have been a black man, African-American, if you will, back in the big city. Up here they as soon call me colored or worse. You can call me Mr. Wright."

Rook nodded. "I'd like a walk through, Mr. Wright."

"You got something to say to my members, they got the right to have me there. And you got to wear a hard hat."

"Deal."

The steward finished his coffee. "Then we better get a move on."

Wright took Rook down the fire stairs, where two workers were catching a smoke. "Break time," one of them said.

The shop steward nodded.

"You 'the man'?" Lucas asked.

"Fair is fair, Mr. ex-policeman. I see they give management a fair day, I see management gives them a fair shake." He handed Rook a yellow safety hat.

"Even Ms. Charney."

"She's alright unless you embarrass her. Lady got to show she's got the biggest dick in the place."

They went into the Loose Room, where broken cases were reboxed and smaller orders readied for shipping. "Somebody orders the bars or the powder, 'Pounds-On,' 'Pounds-Off,' whatever, we see they get what they want. The chains, they buy big, we ship them only by the pallet, which is minimum twenty-four cases. The little stores, gyms, healthfood places, we send them whatever they want, private label and all."

A man in a baseball hat without the brim nodded as Wright came in from the packing room. Two checkers were counting out the loads stacked in the corner.

"Six beauty, two 'on's,' three 'off's.'"

"Check," his partner in the blue apron said.

Wright and Lucas Rook went through the packing room, where the big machine folded boxes, set in the packages of bars, and sent them down the line.

"I'll take you to the mixing room if you want," the steward said. "But you got to put on a gown and mask."

"Going to make it harder for you to piss in my ear?"

Wright turned to face him. "That's just the kind of police talk I'm talking about. I love it. I do. Other than that, I don't know what you're getting at."

"I'm getting at your insurance carrier sent me to take a look at the risk down here. Seems working around here is a risky business."

"Let's 'gown-up,' you would say," the shop steward said with a smile. He looked at his watch. "Now they be running protein powder. It gets mixed in all kinds of things, the shakes, tabs, bars. You won't be able to remember it all, whey protein, you know from Little Miss Muffet, curds and whey, that's from milk, soy protein, lecithin, calcium caseinate." He looked up on the wall. "This run going to be chocolate, with cocoa powder, we get that in burlap bags, and maltodextrin for sweetness." He handed Rook a pair of cloth slippers. "Got to cover up your brogans."

They went inside the mixing room. Everyone wore gowns and goggles. A fine brown powder covered everything. A steady hum made talking useless as the ingredients came in and the mixers turned. The steward brought one of the girls outside. "Where's Holdsworth?" the steward asked.

A nervous girl with her hair wrapped up took the plugs from her ears. "He went home. His kid's sick."

"He clock out?"

The girl nodded and put her plugs back in.

"You got a lot of that around here, shop steward," Rook said.

"I don't get involved in people's private lives, Mr. Policeman."

Wright looked at his watch again. "Time for me to 'chow-down,' or 'lunch-up,' as you might say. I'll walk you back out and you can have a nice day."

"You got anything about the people dying around here, Mr. Wright? Or you going to leave it up to me what I report back to the insurance company?"

"You can report back what you want, Mr. Rook. You want to know about dying around here, you just keep your eye out for 'the brothers' you keep snooping around. Now have that nice day."

Rook wanted to get over to the Holiday Inn to check his messages back at his office and write up what he had so far. Maybe he could get another two full days out of Oneonta, stretch it to three if he scheduled his interviews right. Maybe run up to the Hall of Fame on the clock. Getting over to see the victims' families and the health examiner would be easy. The doctor and the other employees might or might not be. He'd save the sex harasser for last and squeeze the funeral director in somewhere. When Lucas got down to his car, he saw that all four tires were flat.

The Holiday Inn was five blocks away, and his leg was stiffening up from the walk-through at the Bottle House. Rook saw a gas station on the next corner.

"You fix flats?" Rook asked the cashier.

"Me, I just make change." He relit his cigar.

"You got a mechanic?"

"Nope."

"You got two bays over there with cars up on the lifts," Lucas told him. "I expect you got somebody who can fix a tire."

The cashier blew a smoke ring. "He's a sublet. Besides, he's off today."

"How convenient."

"We aim to please," the cashier said. "Stop in anytime."

The town was getting on his nerves. Rook walked across the street to the Dunkin' Donuts.

The proprietor was Indian. His entire family worked with him, covered with flag pins. The place had more memorabilia than any sports bar in New York.

Ramesh Patel came over and took his order. He looked sleepless.

"Rough times?" Lucas asked him.

"Everything's fine, sir."

"I bet it is." Rook handed over his card. "I'll be staying over at the Holiday Inn the next couple of days. Anybody give you a hard time, slash your tires, whatever, give me a call."

Patel tried to show indifference. Rook took his coffee and two sugars and sat in the window. A truck like Turkey Neck's drove by. Either him or the "brothers" he'd been warned about. Whoever it was, he'd get a face to face with them and they wouldn't like it.

An extra twenty at the Holiday Inn got a tow truck over and a promise he'd have a new rental car by 6 PM. The room was clean and cool. Lucas stretched out on one of the beds and called back for his messages. Attorney Warren Phelps placing a three-hundred-dollar call to say nothing was new with the United States Attorney. Grace calling to say, "Hope to see you soon."

Rook changed his socks and went down to the bar. Another "Patel" poured drinks. He had none of the fear the dothead at the Dunkin' Donuts had. Free drinks work wonders. "Call me Pat," he said.

Lucas had a cold beer and some peanuts. A built girl with blotchy skin sat at the bar.

"You looking for a good time?" Pat asked.

"If I am, you'll be the first to know. How's the dining room?"

"Open twenty-four hours, like my niece here."

Rook finished his beer and left a dollar. "Turn it down a notch or two, Gandhi, before somebody runs you in behind your pimping."

Lucas went upstairs. He hung his trousers over the desk and sat for a while in a hot bath with his .38 on the soap dish. He toweled off, then fell asleep.

                    ❧   ❧   ❧

Calvin Treaster stood in the loft in the rear of Heinsel's Lumber, his bald head almost touching the angled rafters, his bare chest glistening with sweat and marked with the scar from his neck to his waist. Bill Gamon and Big Earl Joost and six others all branded with the same half-moon stood below him, their eyes looking up as if to heaven.

Calvin Treaster raised his arms. "We are the Brothers of the Half-Moon. It came to me as clear as day on 9-11 what this sign on me was," he said as he pointed to the huge mark on his belly and then the brand on his arm. "I was born at the foot of the Henry Hudson Bridge, and this mark being the name of Henry Hudson's ship that found New York on 9-11 three hundred years ago. It came to me as clear as day when them buildings fell and the sky was black with smoke.

"The rich men sent Henry Hudson out four times like an arrow in the night. Then they betrayed him and he was set adrift from the Half-Moon with eight others. Sent to die and die they did, them Brothers of the Half-Moon, so the rich could fill this land with the niggers and the Jews. It's them traitors and that greed that brought our country down, and it's us that's sent to take revenge."

Calvin Treaster came down the ladder from his loft, his hands still shaking, the wattle on his neck waving back and forth. "It's all wrong, this country going to rot and drugs. The queers and the chinks. Even the coloreds running things. That's why we put that poison in them protein bars. We going to pay them back, the ones who ruined what was ours."

"The Bottle House," said Big Earl Joost. "The nigger and the dyke is running things."

Billy Gamon walked back and forth.

"They killed John Wayne in Hollywood," said a man whose name was Bute. "And they got Mr. Heston all poisoned sick at the NRA."

Calvin Treaster put his John Deere hat back on and covered up his scars. "Them New York Jews got one of their spies up here."

"I seen him talking to Wesley Wright and then Jack Moore. He tried his sneaky shit on me," said Earl.

"Came in to watch us in the mixing room, but I poured that powder in a couple of days ago like you told me," said Lazy Eye. "So there was nothing for him to see."

"I seen him all about our town, my brothers, all New York like," Cal Treaster said. "Eatin' in one hotel, sleeping in the other. Acting like he was a spy from a foreign country."

"We'll break him up," said Big Earl Joost.

"And cover him with lime," said the funeral director, whose name was Swain.

Turkey Neck dropped Billy Gamon off and went back home. His three dogs ran alongside his truck as he came up the unpaved drive. There was no light inside because no one waited there for him.

Peanut's mother ran off with a man sold bubble wrap she met when he came in to where she worked. Calvin Treaster had meant to hunt them down. Then she called to say that she wasn't coming back and that when she got where she was going, she'd send for her Peanut, who belonged with her, which was where the bright lights were and not in no hick town.

Calvin Treaster heated coffee water in an enamel pan. He had cooked the poison in his kitchen, learning the recipe from a book he ordered from the back of a survival magazine. Everybody worked at the dye house knew that castor mash was poison. But then the federal government made it illegal to grow that natural crop so we would have to send our money to foreigners to bring it back in.

He had bought the beans from two mail order garden supply stores and had them sent to separate P.O. boxes. Then he only needed lye and acetone, which he bought right down at the hardware store. He used some glass jars, tweezers, and some coffee filters and followed the recipe until he had the white ricin powder.

Calvin threw away his rubber gloves and the mask he brought home from the dye house. Then he put the poison in the jewelry box his wife had left behind before he gave it to Duffy to put in those bars in the mixing room.

Calvin Treaster knew it was meant to be, him making that white powder from the castor mash they couldn't make anymore and him being born with that scar at the foot of the Henry Hudson Bridge. And him being the one that got the Brothers of the Half Moon together to set things right.

CHAPTER 15

Rudy Knoll had been a thief from as long as he could remember. His earliest memory was taking a blue stuffed elephant from his babysitter's house. Other than that, the thing he remembered most from his childhood was when they started calling him "Fatboy."

Being called Fatboy and deserving it had its bad effect on Rudy Knoll, but it was his illiteracy that compelled him to live as a thief. He stole everything: dogs, pies, tools, furniture from windows, the bingo receipts of a volunteer fire company.

Fatboy Knoll's skills developed over time, but not without notice. His accomplishments earned him a stay in state prison for making off with a load of toilet seats. His pathological belief that once he stole something, it was his, also resulted in his termination from the Bottle House and his name being on Lucas Rook's list.

When Ms. Charney noticed her right rear tire had gone flat, Rudy Knoll had come jiggling over to lend a hand.

"Thank you, however…" she started. But he was already popping his trunk to remove the pneumatic jack, which had previously been the property of a gas station outside of Cooperstown.

While Rudy loosened the lug nuts of her SUV, Ms. Charney noticed the leaf blower from which Fatboy had not altogether removed the factory's markings. That brought a prompt audit of the maintenance room, which revealed the absence of a pneumatic drill, welder's torch, and several small power tools.

Two days of surveillance ordered by the head of HR at $35 per hour generated a cinematic masterpiece of Rudy selling the welder's torch and mask to Janusky's Bodyshop down the road. With that videotape and her view of the leafblower, Ms. Chaney felt completely justified in installing a camera in the maintenance shed. It took three days before Rudy Knoll was caught rolling out cans of roofing muck.

When confronted, Rudy brought forth what he considered his charm, which originated from the fact that an aunt had once described his chubby cheeks as "cherubic." Ms. Charney was immune, so he tried to bully her.

"I'm going to put a lawsuit on you and the whole company," he said. "False arrest and slander on my good name."

She ignored him altogether.

"Got a lawyer from over in Monroe. I'm going to own this place," Rudy said.

"You do that, Mr. Knoll," Ms. Charney said. "You just do that."

"And the union, we'll close this place down," he told her.

"I think not, Rudy. Mr. Wright and I have already had a chance to sit down together and watch the tapes of you. The universal opinion is that you are slime."

He turned to go.

"Oh, just a minute, dear. Security will be here to walk you to the gate lest you find a box of paper clips or a copy machine to be irresistible."

"I never…"

"You never did an honest day's work, Rudy Knoll. Goodbye."

Fatboy moved three times after that, but it was easy for Lucas Rook to find him with the info from his personnel file. The driver's license numbers led Rook to Cornelia Place, a string of flat two-story houses with garages in the back.

Lucas sat outside of Knoll's place for two hours watching the people come and go. An old man in a walker being taken out by his dutiful son. A pizza delivery being answered by a man wearing only a shirt. Little girls with matching coats going out to play.

He looked at his watch, though years on the job told him without fail that it was coffee time. Since no way was this a thermos job, he pulled around Cornelia Place and out on to the highway to the Krispy Kreme two miles west.

A seat opened up at the counter. A uniform from the Orange County Sheriff's office sat two stools down.

"You mind we change seats?" Rook asked the patron in between them. When the man hesitated, Lucas tinned him.

The deputy looked up from his newspaper. Rook flashed his old NYPD badge a second time.

"Up from the City, looking for this mutt," he said.

The deputy, whose name was Oberholser, was new on the job, but eager. "What the mutt do?" he tried.

"Scammed a priest, Obie, and made off with the bingo dough."

"You kidding me? What parish?"

"Perp's name is Rudy Knoll."

Deputy Oberholser put down his fork. "You kidding me? Rudy from over at the Home Depot? He's assistant manager in the plumbing department. Helped me with the right flange for this job I'm doing at my mother-in-law's."

Rook's coffee came with a pair of fine-looking donuts. "One and the same, Deputy. They better check their inventory. This boy's got sticky fingers. Been jammed up more than a toilet at a Giants game."

Obie shook his head. "He works over at the Home Depot, 8 to 4. It's right down the road here. I'll tell my sergeant when I check in."

"You're good, partner," Rook said. He paid for both of them and swung over to the Home Depot.

Fatboy worked the store in an extra large jacket with deep pockets. Lucas watched him come out with a lunch box and his jacket draped over his arm. Knoll's station wagon was filled with junk, a perfect cover for any new items, from ceiling fans to copper tubing. He drove around the parking lot and stopped at a large green dumpster. In went a bag of trash. Out came a bag of light bulbs. A regular klepto.

Lucas stayed two cars behind and waited in a shopping center while Fatboy did his food shopping. Probably had a dozen steaks in his pants.

Rook followed him to Cornelia Place and parked across the street. He got out of his car and walked up right behind the klepto as he opened the front door.

A thin black man with processed hair greeted them both. "And just who might you be?" he asked Lucas Rook.

Rudy turned around and was face to face with Rook as he was pushed backwards into his house. "Well, I be the man who's going to lock you two girls up." He flashed his badge.

"You'll have to show more I.D. than that," the black man said.

"Don't know who you are, but you favor Diana Ross. You'll get all the I.D. you want, Diana, when I book you for conspiracy and receiving stolen goods. Meantime, why don't we just sit down. You two love birds will have plenty of time to keep your mouth open at 'the Tombs.'"

Fatboy looked like he was going to cry.

"Sit down, Rudolph Knoll," Rook said. "You got a big problem. If you're smart you'll sit down and do what I tell you."

"And if I don't?" he dared.

"Then you'll find yourself in Ossining and by the time you get out, your friend here will be just another lonely fag."

Fatboy and Diana sat down together on the sofa.

"What it looks like to me is we got a kingpin and his queen of a bigtime burglary ring. The State Police think it's maybe quarter of a mil a month."

Diana had his long hand over his mouth, and Rudy had turned pale. "It's not like that," Fatboy said.

"But me," Rook went on. "My interests are more local." He paused. "And more severe." Lucas opened his jacket to show the butt of his sidearm. "Let's go downstairs, Rudy. I'm sure your basement is a regular Home Depot."

In the basement, Rook saw boxes of toilet paper, tools, cans of paint, plastic milk cartons filled with faucets, air fresheners, and rolls of tape.

"Not very discriminating, are we, Rudolph. If it's not tied down you boost it."

"That's not right."

"Absolutely it is. Which is why I figure you for a klepto fag, which to me could add up you do homicide." He could see Knoll's legs buckle.

"I never…"

"You got caught on tape. You killed two men, maybe three at the Bottle House. Edna Charney, the HR Director over there said you tried to whack her too, tried to run her over. Nice lady, Edna."

Lucas heard a noise on the steps and turned. It was Fatboy's girlfriend, and he had a kitchen knife in his hand.

Rook stepped back and triangulated them with his .45. "Now put that knife down, Diana Ross, and come on down the steps. I'm going to count to two and then I'm going to shoot Rudolph in the dick. Then I'm going to shoot you in the face."

He set the knife down, turned, and ran.

"So much for the sanctity of marriage, Mr. Knoll. Now give it up."

"I don't understand," Fatboy said. There were tears running down his cherubic cheeks. "I take things, I boosted a lot of shit from where I worked. I always do. They caught me and they ran me out."

"Save the drama for your mama, Mr. Knoll." Lucas put the barrel of his weapon to Rudy's head.

"One of them boys that died was my nephew. You fucked up somehow. You cop to it, I let you live. You hold out on me, you're dead." Rook slowly cocked the hammer.

Fatboy crapped himself. The smell was overwhelming. "You got cases of toilet paper down here, Rudolph. Clean yourself up."

Lucas went upstairs and outside. The black man was leaning against the car crying.

"Go back inside," Rook told him. "Your boyfriend needs some attention."

Rudy Knoll was a sick fag thief whose whole life was crimes. But no way was he involved with the deaths at the Bottle House. Rook looked at his watch. He'd grab some lunch, then pay a visit to the next one on his list.

The bartender at the Holiday Inn had told Lucas there was a decent diner on 209 and that Canno's served lunch. He'd get a burger and hopefully a good cup of coffee, and then pay Jack Curran a visit. He wanted his strength if he was going to be looking at an ex-boxer with a bad temper.

The diner had good coffee and fresh made pea soup, but the burger was dry. Lucas got a roll of quarters for each hand and pulled away.

Rook's first real fight had been on his first day on foot patrol. It was life and death because if it went bad, he would lose his ability to do his job, lose his service revolver and maybe wind up dead. Skillet Baynard hanging outside Rankin's Barbershop, all 6'3", 230 lbs. of him. Head as hard as iron. Skillet saw Lucas coming up the block and he meant to wolf him.

"What you doin' on my block, Mr. Pig?" he said.

"I'm here for the New York Police Department," Rook said to him. "To serve the citizens of this fine city."

"You an occupying mother fucker," Skillet said.

Lucas had listened well to Jim McCullagh before he went out to walk his beat. He brought his nightstick as hard as he could to Skillet's shin. The bone broke audibly and the wolf went down.

"Good morning to you, neighbor," Lucas said. "I hope that we meet again."

There were a couple of times when Kirk and Lucas rode the same blue and white that they fought back to back. And there was the time that he got cold-cocked flat and would have gotten stomped to death except for Ray Tuzio, who was there and used his blackjack fast.

Then the job changed. The bad guys weren't afraid to fight a cop, and the cops were afraid to use their sticks. Now that he was older and private, Rook always moved first and used every cruel trick he could.

CHAPTER 16

It didn't make any sense that somebody who used his fists to settle things would be poisoning anybody. Women, family members did that kind of thing. He once caught a case with Tuzio, a whackjob mother poisoned three kids with ginger snaps over her ten-year-old's Halloween costume. Seems nobody but her precious was going to be Bart Simpson or whatever. But on this job, Mrs. Politte was writing checks, so everybody got the nice long look that Rudy Knoll got, including Jack Curran.

No one answered at Curran's address. The little row house looked abandoned. The yard was a mess, a pile of tires, two front doors, cinder blocks, bricks and an old stove. A chain hung from the tree at Curran's place where he probably hung a heavy bag.

Rook tried the next house down. A fat lady in a sleeveless housedress opened the door.

"Irish move away. I'm Ida. 'Ida, Ida. Sweeter than apple cider.'"

"You have a street number, dear?"

She took a lipstick from her housecoat and did her lips up pink. "You and Jack Curran get along?"

Ida jiggled and licked her pink lips. "I like to lick the candy stick. He liked the jelly roll. You want a cup of tea?"

"Got to talk to Jack about his benefits from the Bottle House. He got some leave pay coming. You got the number for me?" He moved up to the next step. "I'll tell Jack you're asking for him."

Ida tried a little frown. "Irish and me didn't part on such good terms."

"He rough you up?"

"Jack Curran's got a temper is all."

"You got an address for me, dear. I'll stop back."

Ida pulled on herself. "I like to lick the candy stick," she said. "I like to lick it up."

"I'll tell Jack you said hello."

Way too much information, Rook told himself. He went next door on the other side. The blinds were drawn. Lights were on inside. Rook tried the bell and when no one answered, he knocked.

"Jack Curran moved away to be near the bus," said the toothless man who opened the door.

"Went to Hollywood," called a voice from inside. "Going to do a movie with Gary Cooper."

The toothless man laughed out loud, his shoulders going up and down.

"And Susan Hayward," said the voice from inside.

"Ain't she something, mister. Agnes, you been smoking something?"

"You got an address for Jack Curran? I'm from the Bottle House to talk to him about his benefits."

"And Humphrey Bogart. And George Raft too," she called.

"Going to be a helluva show, neighbor," Rook told him.

"Going to be a helluva show, Aggie, he says."

"And Van Johnson in a supporting role," Rook said.

The man at the front door laughed so hard that tears were in his eyes.

"You help me out, neighbor, I tell you and your wife a Hollywood secret."

The man stopped laughing. "You got a deal," he said. He went back inside and came out with an address.

"The wife says to tell you she wants Lee J. Cobb in a cameo role. What's your Hollywood secret, we want to know."

"Randolph Scott was a queer. Wore dresses. So was Raymond Burr," Rook said.

"You're joshing me," said the toothless man. "You surely are."

Rook drove over to the new address. There was a bus stop across the street. An unmarked van drove by. He wrote down the plate, an old habit from the PD. Vans were the favorite for the child snatchers and rapists. Hundreds of them, thousands on the prowl. Everybody on the job knew that.

Lucas watched Curran's house. No mail box, dirty windows, the garage in the back had a broken lock. He sat for an hour, then checked his watch. Rook took his map out and drove north on 28 to Cooperstown. He'd figure out how to bill it after.

Lucas Rook had been at the Hall of Fame as a kid with his uncle Carl, who had sold furniture with Stan Musial's brother. Everybody did Stan the Man's stance when they were batting lefty in the street.

Cooperstown could have turned into Disneyland or worse, but it still was like a small town used to be, except that every store sold baseball stuff. Vintage hats, Reggie Jackson shirts they signed themselves, and now dozens of things with NYPD and the firefighters. The twin towers and Reggie Jackson on an ice tea glass. Never underestimate the American spirit.

It was coffee time and there was a little place between The Dug Out and the Tenth Inning. The Home Plate had switched to serving lunch, but there was a good old-fashioned coffee maker behind the counter. You served latte to Rook and you got jacked.

The countergirl poured him a cup of coffee when he first sat down.

"My dad was on the job for thirty years. I know the look. You're from the City."

"That I am. Your dad?"

"The Utica PD. Then he got sick, CMT. It's a neurological disease like Lou Gehrig's only it don't get any publicity, except now that that basketball player got it who was with the Nets. We got fresh made pie. Apple crumb and blueberry."

Lucas stirred his cup and stretched his leg. "Apple crumb is good. This your family's place?"

She came back with the pie. "Daddy got sick and mom ran off with a boy half her age. She met him on the Garden State. Guess he rubbed her palm while he took the tolls."

The pie was good. Rook watched the people going by. Fathers and sons. Fat men wearing little league hats. Old timers remembering when. The Mick flying down to first and roofing it from both sides. Willie's catch. Good stuff.

"You remind me of my dad," the countergirl said.

"That's nice," he said and left two one's.

The Baseball Hall of Fame was down the street. The plaques were first. Johnny Van Der Meer, who threw two straight no-hitters forever. The Big Cat, Johnny Mize. And endless loop of the Babe, never showing the cancer-stricken man the Yankees turned their backs on.

At the "Who's on First" display, Rook saw an old friend walking by. The John Deere hat was gone, but it was him, turkey neck and all. Turkey Neck had a ladder in his hand.

There was a crash of glass from the gift shop and the manager came out, a flatnosed girl in a retro uniform. "Cal, can you give me a hand?" she called.

He put his ladder down and went in. Lucas followed.

"I'm sorry," said a woman in a Dodgers hat. "We'll pay for it," she offered. "Say you're sorry, Jay."

"It's alright," the manager said. "It happens all the time. Don't it, Cal?"

"Don't it, Cal?" Lucas added.

Cal Treaster nodded.

Rook walked in close. "You want me to hold the dustpan, Cal?"

Turkey Neck shook his head. Then the manager came over.

"You didn't get any shards on you?" she asked.

"Shards?" Rook said.

"Fragments, broken pieces. I used to be a teacher."

"No, I'm fine. Cal here is a big help."

She walked away.

Rook leaned closer. Treaster moved away.

"You don't like people getting close. Most cons don't."

"I ain't no con."

"You on my tail again, you going to be. You got something to say, you say it now."

"Why don't you ride on back to Manhattan?" said Calvin Treaster.

"Did you say 'while I still can'? Because then you got a big problem."

"I got work to do," Treaster said.

"I got my eye on you," Rook said. "You twitch in the wrong direction, you're going to wish you were never born."

Rook took his time in the Golden Days, Heroes Then and Forever. Then left for Jack Curran, through the little park, past another statue of James Fenimore Cooper. Two black boys were sitting on the metal lap, posing for their father's photo.

Lucas drove back down Route 28. On the way he called in to pick up his messages, somebody flying in to New York who wanted post 9-11 security, and Sid Rosen.

When Rook got back to Curran's house there was still nobody home. The toothless man was coming down the street walking his collie on a leash. "Come on, Edward G," he said.

Lucas sat for an hour and a half and then pulled away. The old days he could hold his pee like a camel or piss in a mason jar. First thing he learned when he was in the cruiser, always bring a mason jar. McCullagh told him don't be pouring it on nobody's lawn, it'll kill the grass. Don't play no pranks, we seen them all.

There was a gas station down the road. Rook took a leak, then drove in as the bus came up the other way. Jack Curran got off. He had his hands wrapped fighter's style in machinist's tape.

The driver's license in his personnel file didn't do him justice. Irish Jack's face showed he'd been in the ring, a thick neck like Jerry Quarry's, square head, strong arms. He tucked his chin in when he walked. Rook took his blackjack out and stood outside of punching range.

"Ms. Charney sent me."

Curran made two fists. "They shitcanned me."

"You broke somebody's jaw, Jack."

"Called me a bum."

"I saw you fight once in Sunnyside Gardens. You could bring it, Irish Jack."

"And take it too."

Jack Curran took the cigarette from behind his ear. By the way he lit up, Rook could tell he was nearly blind.

"She just wanted to know how you were doing."

"Whatever," Jack said. "I'm getting my social security checks regular anyhow. She can drop dead."

❦   ❦   ❦

Poison had been Webster Clark's life and would be his death. First sitting in the Vietnam rain. Then the Agency had sent him to the Dugway Proving Ground, locked in by mountains and the Great Salt Lake Desert. Eight hundred thousand acres with armed patrols and the sky shut down.

Inside, poisoned bombs and shells exploded from a tower thirty stories high. Dugway tested death. Fifty years of chemical and biological weapons. When General Creasy retired, they killed a thousand guinea pigs as his salute.

There were concrete buildings set in the mountains and twenty Ph.D.'s. Families growing up there, watching the foxes on Five Mile Hill, the children wearing badges when they reached ten. Everyone watched the birds. Pigeons bit by gas do the same as humans do. They die fast.

Clark worked the labs at Dugway Proving Ground: the CCTF, Bushnell, and the Baker lab eight miles away where the air was burned and scrubbed before it was released. He learned about ricin, anthrax, Ebola, Q fever, Sarin, and VX. Arsenals for the left, the right, the nationalists, the separatists, the paranoid, and the grandiose. The armies of the light, the armies of the night.

Webster Clark made notes on the man that Lucas Rook had met and then drove away. With Rook's help, he was defining the role of the Brothers of the Half Moon and their poison game. He let the detective think he was making moves, but it was Webster Clark who ran the game.

CHAPTER 17

Rook had two doctors to see. Dr. Jaimie Mesoros from the hospital and Shirley Roy, the family practitioner. Except for the fact that the meter was running, two doctors in one day was two too many.

Mesoros wasn't due in until after 8 PM, so he drove out to see Dr. Roy. The front lawn of the converted twin homes had been turned into a parking lot. The modern sign out front read, "Oneonta Family Practice, P.C." The smaller one, "Shirley E. Roy, M.D."

Lucas went up the wide steps. The inside had been modernized and the waiting room was full. There was a curving wall that went three quarters up with clowns on it. A kid's cough came from the other side as did, "Didn't I tell you to cover your mouth?"

Two obese women sat at the front desk. "May I help you?" said the one in the yellow smock. "Can I help you?" said the one whose smock was pink.

"Yes and no," Rook said. "I do not have an appointment, and I would like to see Dr. Roy."

"Pharmaceutical reps are seen on Thursday."

Rook leaned in close to the two of them and showed his badge.
"Oh," said the yellow one.

"Oh," said the pink. "I'd better get Mrs. McClory."

An old woman came up behind him, walking slowly. Her sneeze
was wet on the back of his neck. Lucas turned around. Her eyes
were dim. A crooked man held her arm.

Mrs. McClory came out of the back. She wore a lime green suit.
Her hair and make-up were perfect. "Will you come this way?" she
asked.

Rook followed her walk that hinted at undulation. Her office
was neat and to the point. No pictures of kids to go with her wedding band. Degree from Syracuse. A picture of her with Hillary
Clinton.

"May I see your identification?" She had a yellow pad and pen
conspicuously on her desk meaning, I write things down. I mean
business.

Rook produced the private ID. "I have been retained on behalf
of Centurion Insurance Company."

Mrs. McClory waited for him to go on. He didn't. "And how
can we help you?" she said.

"By my talking to Dr. Roy for fifteen minutes so that I don't
have to tie you all up with subpoenas and the good doctor with a
deposition the night before Christmas."

June McClory's fair complexion reddened. "I see no need for
contentiousness, Mr. Rook." She took a deep breath. "And as you
may know, this practice is one of a hundred owned by Northeastern
Health Systems…"

"And you have two zillion lawyers on retainer." He tried a smile.

"Actually only one zillion. You know almost everything you're
probably going to ask is privileged and I will have to sit in." She ran
Dr. Roy's schedule up on her screen. "She's booked solid. I could

move her lunch to 2:30, then fit you in."

"Thirty minutes for lunch. Kind of stingy."

"Good practice management." She smiled back.

"I'll grab a cup of coffee," Lucas said.

"There's a nice place around the corner, Polly's Tearoom. They make their own sweets."

Rook got up. "I prefer something a little more institutional. See you then."

He went back through the waiting room. People were backed up to the front doors. The parking lot was crowded. Cars double-parked.

A white station wagon went up the driveway next door. A round-faced man came out of the house in overalls. He had a white German shepherd on a short chain. "You get on out of here," he yelled. "You think you own the world. This is my world." The man in the overalls pulled hard on the leash. The driver of the station wagon tried to back out, but lost control and pulled across his lawn.

The lady panicked and cut her wheels the wrong way, backing across the grass. Lucas walked over. There were two boys in the back seat. One of them had a nose bleed.

The round-faced man came back down his driveway with a shotgun. Rook met him halfway. "You her husband?" the man said. "I got some for you too."

"I'm nobody's husband," Rook told him. "Go on back inside, neighbor, before you piss all over your life."

"You don't scare me, mister."

"Yes I do," Rook told him. "Now you go on back inside and have a cold beer while I get you the lady's insurance information. You make a claim, you'll do real good. You make this hard, it's going to rain trouble for you." Rook's hand was at his weapon. "I'll forget you walking out here with that Ithaca constitutes a felony. Now go have a beer."

The man in the overalls thought about it, then went back up his driveway. He looked over his shoulder for effect, but he kept on going.

Rook walked over to the station wagon on the grass. The woman was crying and trying to light a cigarette. The boys in the back were crying too.

"What's your name?" he asked.

"Tom," said the one without the nosebleed. "He's Jerry. He gets bloody noses, but he's okay."

Lucas leaned in the car. "You take them in. I'll park this for you."

"You carjacking us?"

"I don't think so, lady. You want to sit here or pull up onto that man's porch, you go right ahead."

The woman shook her head and let Rook take over. He looked at his watch. The opportunity for coffee, even with "sweets," had passed him by. Lucas pulled the car onto the street and went back into the doctor's office. The heavy lady in the pink smock had been replaced by a heavy lady in a yellow smock. They looked like a gigantic two-headed chicken.

"Your insurance card," the new head said.

"He's here to see Dr. Roy," the other said. "Mrs. McClory gave him an appointment for three o'clock."

"It's not three o'clock yet. Please have a seat."

Rook didn't move. Mrs. McClory came out of her office. "We're running late. It will be another twenty-five minutes or so."

"I'll wait."

She walked over, surrounded by her perfume.

"I never made it to that coffee," Rook said.

"I have just what the doctor ordered," she said. He wondered whether the perfume meant she was talking about something else.

"It's a challenge," she said in her office, "to balance health care delivery and corporate accountability."

"I bet."

June McClory offered the coffee.

"Black is good," he told her.

She adjusted her watch. "I'm here from Los Angeles."

"The 'left coast.' You don't miss it?"

The intercom rang. "Dr. Roy can see you now." Mrs. McClory with the fine walk and the splash of perfume led the way.

Dr. Shirley Roy met them in a treatment room. She was dressed in a green smock with bunnies on it and was sitting in a wheelchair.

"Nice to get off my feet for a bit. Mrs. McClory says you have some questions for me. And I cooperate with my practice manager whenever possible."

"I appreciate that," Rook said. "I'm here on behalf of Centurion Insurance Company, looking at some cases of fatal gastric illness."

"There are issues of confidentiality, Mr. Rook."

"We appreciate that," Mrs. McClory said.

"Arnetta Holmes and Jackie Moore, you were their general practitioner."

Dr. Roy nodded.

"They died of acute gastric illness," Rook went on. "Is there anything you can tell me about their past medical history?"

The doctor looked at her watch. "First, Mr. Rook, I do not have their charts. I have access only when there is an appointment. Second, I have hundreds of patients so I have no independent recollection. Third, I have patients to see."

Dr. Roy got up and left.

Lucas followed Mrs. McClory's perfume back to her office.

"Maybe we can reschedule this," she said. "I'll have the records available if you have the proper Releases for Information."

"That would be fine," Rook said. "Shall I call you?"

"You can call me June."

"I'll do that, June. I'll do that."

Lucas knew that there wasn't a county office in the world that did any work at all after four-thirty. After four o'clock was fifty-fifty.

He drove over to the Public Health office. With a little luck he'd get a stack of paperwork to digest and a couple more people to talk to. The clerk at Public Health looked Mohawk.

Rook flashed his gold ID. "We didn't get your numbers."

"What numbers are that?" the Mohawk asked.

Lucas shook his head. "That's even worse."

"Computers are down, Mister. Only numbers you can find around here are in the phone book."

"I'll be back," Rook said. "Meanwhile, since you seem like a good guy, I'll forget you not only didn't get the data, but that you were acting like a smart ass."

CHAPTER 18

Hawkeye's was another one of the theme restaurants around Oneonta. The sign outside said, "Your Pathfinder to Good Food." Maybe all the help wore leather stockings. Rook hoped not. No need for Christopher Street in the country.

The parking lot was mostly empty. Upstate folks didn't eat out much during the week unless they were tourists or on an expense account. There were two trucks parked in the back. One of them looked like it was Turkey Neck's. The next time the two of them met was not going to be a party.

He scoped the place before he presented himself to the hostess. One way in for patrons. A side door out. Something in the back for deliveries.

The hostess had emerald eyes and long cool legs.

"You should be wearing leather stockings," he told her.

She looked at him.

"When did you move up here, green eyes?"

"You could tell?"

"Queens, Astoria most likely," Rook said.

"I'm Terry." She smiled and shifted her weight on those great legs.

A middle-aged couple came in walking close together. They separated when Rook glanced at them.

Terry walked him to his table.

"A lady not his wife," Lucas said.

"How'd you know, Astoria? You just *knew*, right?"

"As sure as I am the Yanks play in the Bronx."

A family with two kids stood at the reservation desk.

"I bet you know the exact street and all. You read minds?" she said. "I hope you do," she added as she walked away.

The server came over. He should not have been wearing leather anything. It was Patel, the bartender, from the Holiday Inn.

"How you doin'?" Rook said.

"How you doing?" Pat said, trying to get the accent just right. "My days off, I'm over here. You get dinners you do pretty well, good."

Lucas looked at the menu. "What's good, Pat? The menu's all stupid. 'Pathfinder' burger, whatever. Only thing I've seen worse was over at Canastota. They got everything named after the boxers, Rocky Marciano pasta, and so on."

Pat leaned in. "Canastota? I'm not familiar with the establishment."

"The Boxing Hall of Fame, like you got up the road for baseball in Cooperstown. It's in Canastota, maybe an hour away."

Patel nodded. "Like Muhammad Ali, right. I don't know much more than that. I work. Go to school, study to be a nurse. Same hours, but big bucks. And I'll look very good in the uniforms."

Rook nodded in appreciation at the attempt at humor. "What's good, Pat?"

"The meat is very good. It comes in daily. The prime rib queen size is the best value. You get the salad bar and dessert. The second beer's on me."

Lucas waited for the first cold one to arrive. "You know who owns the truck out there in the back?"

"I do not. I only rarely drive my Toyota Corolla 2-door into the parking lot."

The beer was perfect in a chilled glass. Rook called into his office. Nothing new. Then he picked up the messages from his apartment. There were two calls from Grace four minutes apart. "You're home, pick up," the first one said.

The second was about her cat. "It's me. Faustus went over to your place. I'll leave the slider open. If he brings anything home with him, I'll make him put it back."

Lucas returned her call. The greeting on her message machine played in a bad German accent, "You leave de message at the sound of de tanks rolling through the Poland. Sig Heil!"

Grace picked up when she heard who it was. "I'm okay," she said. "I know you wanted to check on me. Faustie's back. Thank you."

He could hear her lighting a cigarette.

"I thought you quit again, Grace."

"A rat's ass you care. You ever see a fat model? We all smoke."

"I'm glad your cat is back. Everything else alright?"

"You're glad, you prick. I'm worried sick and my Faustie's sunning himself on your terrace."

He finished his beer. "Calm down, Grace. I'm upstate."

"Bullshit. I heard you. That's what we blind folks do. I can hear a pigeon fart a block away."

"Thanks for sharing. You need me, call me on my cell. Meanwhile you keep your sliding door closed."

"Don't go, Lucas."

"Grace, this is a dollar a minute."

"I need you, Lucas Rook, man of mystery. My Ducky's gone."

His salad came. Shredded lettuce and wheels of tomato and onion.

"Buy another one, Grace. I'll buy you one."

"You don't understand. Duk Sung Koh is my hairdresser."

"Grace, my dinner's here."

"Lucas, I'm a gourmet chef. I'll cook for you."

"You got thirty seconds, Grace."

"He needed me to shave."

"Isn't that a fashion thing? Don't some of you modern women…"

Her laugh was genuine. "No, no you ninny. He didn't, I mean I
didn't mean down there. I mean Ducky needs a man."

"You kept me on the phone to do shtick?"

"Next time you're home, don't pretend you're not," she said and
she hung up.

The entrée arrived too rare. Pat took it back, apologizing as if he
had killed the Pope. Lucas ate his salad and more bread than he
wanted to. Patel brought him a shrimp cocktail. "Compliments of
the management."

"As if they knew, Pat."

The meat came back. The plate was too hot, so Lucas started on
the baked potato and his second beer. Patel offered dessert, a piece
of apple pie, homemade, not the kind that had been turning in the
plastic lazy susan for a week, but Rook let it go. He wondered whether
Pat would do "the dinner is on management, I get a fat tip" thing.
Anybody worth a shit in the food business could rob the place blind,
which is why Joe Oren was at his place a million hours a week.

Lucas put the dinner on his AMEX and drove over to the hospital to interview Dr. Mesoros. Professional pride dictated that he use
an indirect approach. He'd see how the good doctor reacted to a
representative from her malpractice carrier.

The administrative offices were closed, but there was a large
receptionist desk in the main lobby. The woman behind the desk

was on her cell phone.

"Dr. Mesoros," he said.

She was busy talking about whether Dr. Carter was as good-looking as George Clooney and thank God he had stopped drinking.

"Dr. Mesoros," he repeated.

"I'm sorry, Doctor," she said. "Can I help you?"

"No, dear, I'm not Dr. Mesoros. I'm Dr. Cooper. I'm supposed to meet Dr. Mesoros."

She smiled and called down to the Emergency Room and then to the Charge Nurse. "I'm sorry," she said. "Dr. Mesoros has left for the day. I mean the night."

"That's fine, dear. Sorry to disturb you. Give my regards to St. Elsewhere."

Rook thought about stopping back for that pie and maybe Terry with the long legs, but drove back to the Holiday Inn. He'd write up his daily notes when he got back to the room, which meant that he had ten hours billing. Life was good.

The sour cream from his potato wasn't sitting well, and Lucas wished he had brought some Zantac. He stopped at the vending machine in the hall and got a can of ginger ale and a newspaper.

The hallway was long and clean, but the low ceilings made it feel like he was underground. He could smell a cheap cigar. Never open a door with your hands full. He put the can in his pocket, the paper under his arm and slid the keycard into the lock.

From years on the job, Rook went inside at a sharp angle. The cigar smell was stronger. He ducked and brought his left hand up as the lead pipe crashed into the doorjamb.

Somebody grabbed at his gunhand as he brought his .45 out. Rook lowered his head and rushed like a linebacker, taking the two behind him into the dark room. One of them was big, maybe 250. The other had strong hands.

Lucas wrenched free long enough to make a try for his ankle rig, but the lead pipe took him down. Then the big man grabbed him up. Maybe 6'5". Right-handed.

The voice from behind sounded like Calvin Treaster. "This is the one came looking for you, Jack. Said you were a no good pug. Never was nothing. Now you're a blind freak, he says."

Jack Curran, the pro boxer, going to come with all his hate and shame. The churning rage. "I'm going to break you up," said Curran. "I'm going to beat you blind."

The fighter, Rook told himself, going to come with the left hook first. No need to throw the jab. Lucas tried to push and pull to get some room, but they held him tight. The first one came in hard and low. The liver shot took him down.

It was hard to breathe. Lucas Rook could hear the blind man moving in the dark. "Break you up. Beat you blind," Curran said over and over again.

Rook stayed down. "I'll clean your clock, Jackie boy. They let me go, I'll make you cry."

"Let him go, Cal. Let him go," Jack Curran said.

"Do like I say, Jack. Hurt him bad."

"Fuck him up," said Big Earl.

They straightened Rook up. The next one came on the other side. He felt a rib crack. He dropped as low as he could and this time came up with his ankle gun.

The .38 roared in the small black room. "My foot, my foot," cried Big Earl Joost. Jack Curran turning blind in the dark. Cal Treaster running out the door.

"I'll shoot you dead, Jack," said Lucas Rook.

"I'm better off," said Curran and he came swinging. Earl Joost sat in the bathroom, trying to staunch the bleeding with a towel and crying out for help. Rook saw the tattoo on his right arm.

Blind Jack Curran came forward in the dark, a snorting beast, driving out his angry, futile hands, screaming for his vengeance. Lucas Rook turned on the light and for a moment watched the tragic show. Jack Curran had the same half moon as Big Earl Joost.

Lucas Rook made it to his car, woozy and in pain. Safest place now was the hospital. If he passed out now, they'd grab him up for sure.

As he drove to the ER, the pain in his sides increased. He threw up. Rook made it to the waiting room before he collapsed.

When he opened his eyes, there was an IV in his arm. A beautiful woman crossed the room. "So you're Lucas Rook," she said. "I'm Dr. Mesoros."

"I must be in heaven," Lucas told her.

"Could have been, Mr. Rook."

He tried to sit up, but the pain and dizziness brought him back down.

"The neurologist will be in to see you in the morning. Your skull series came out negative, but it's protocol when there are such post concussive symptoms. I've ordered a CT scan for your internal injuries."

"I was going to stop by and see you, Dr. Mesoros."

She made a notation in his chart. "I only see patients in the Emergency Room, Mr. Rook."

"I'm an investigator. It's about the Moore and Holmes cases..."

"I don't..."

"Your malpractice carrier wanted me to ask you a couple of questions."

"Is there a problem?" Dr. Mesoros asked.

"Not now there isn't. Let's just call this preemptive risk management."

"I don't understand. And I have patients to see. And you're in no condition..."

Rook eased himself up. "I think we'd both rather have this information before a claim is even opened. Once there's a file, it's a mark against you even if it doesn't go anywhere. And every time you renew your policy you have to explain it all over again. This way we get to talk about it off the record first."

Dr. Mesoros called the floor nurse and told her she'd be running behind schedule. She closed the door. "So what you're asking I'm not really answering, right?"

"Right. And I wasn't mugged last night coming out of a hotel bar. You're just cooperating with your insurance carrier as you're supposed to, giving me enough information so some smarmy plaintiff's lawyer will have to stick it where the sun don't shine."

"That I will do. But I really think this should wait."

"There's paper and a pen in my jacket. Let me get this over with quick. It's the least I can do, you taking care of me like you are."

She retrieved the narrow reporter's tablet from his inside pocket and offered her pen.

"Did you test Jackie Moore and Arnetta Holmes?"

"I did. Although without their charts I can't go into specifics."

"No need for that at this point. Do you remember the cases?" He tried to sit up straight.

"Both terminal. Acute gastric illness. I remember that."

"Did the diagnosis go any further?"

"Not as far as I know. Although I wouldn't necessarily know in any case. It depends on a lot of other things how a terminal case is classified." She palpated his flank.

He winced. "Like what?"

"Other cases, hospital policy, hospital politics."

"Were there any other gastric deaths that you know of?"

"I don't recall. The two patients presented with flu-like symptoms. I remember that. Nothing out of the ordinary. Then it just raced ahead, accelerated. The onset was rapid and…"

"Do you have any reason to suspect anything out of the ordinary?"

Dr. Mesoros made a note on his chart. "Not in the slightest. I don't even think a tox screen was ordered."

"Last question, Doc. When is the bass drum in my head going

to stop beating?"

"Why don't you lie back down and get some rest? I'll check back later."

"Good idea, Doc."

She went out and Rook tried to get comfortable. He was just starting to drift off when his beeper went off. He tried to ignore it, but it rang again.

Lucas got out of bed and made it to the closet. It was flashing 9-1-1. He called back to his service. Somebody had beaten Sid Rosen bad.

Rook got dressed and made it to his car. He was woozy, but he had taken worse. His adrenaline would get him home.

CHAPTER 19

The road turned and turned in the slick, black rain. Lucas Rook reached for the lights that were not there. No grille lights flashing, no siren screaming to find his twin brother in the sidewalk blood. His mirrored brother in the mirrored blood.

He pulled over. The girl in the gas station had a black ace tattoo on her hand.

"Gimme the Anacin," Lucas said.

Her other hand had the deuce of hearts. "And fill 'er up?" she asked.

"And fill it up." Rook looked for coffee, but there was none.

"People asking for coffee all the time," she said.

He tore the pack and swallowed the pills dry. His head hurt and he'd been pissing blood. Blind or not, Jack Curran had heavy hands.

Rook stayed in the inside lane, driving with the windows open. He stopped twice to puke. The pus bags upstate weren't going anywhere, and he'd be back to pay them each a visit, and not just for an hourly rate.

Lucas made it to the City and pulled up to St. Vincent's Hospital like he was driving his unmarked. He owned the world with his eyes, and it wasn't worth having.

A short security guard came up. "You can't park there!" he yelled, waving his small hands.

"You don't want to be obstructing, Security Officer Lally. And you don't want my unit here to get a scratch or ding, now do you?"

Rook went into the ER. The waiting room was crowded. A gangbanger with a red bandana sat closest to the door. His left hand was in a bloody shirt. A fat woman wheezed and a man in a cowboy hat rocked back and forth.

There was nobody at the plastic window. Rook went through the swinging doors. A tech came over to wave him off, but Herb Ferry saw him. He was a strong man, who wore his scrubs with the sleeves cut off Ted Kluzewski style. "I thought you were retired, Rook," he said.

"You too, Doc. Thought you'd be in the Hamptons by now simonizing your Ferrari."

"They keep cutting back the reimbursement, I'll be here forever. Let me get you in a room. Looks like you caught a few."

"You got Sid Rosen here. Friend of mine." Lucas found himself looking past Ferry and brought himself back.

"Rusty old boy. They tuned him up pretty good, Lucas. I'm guessing they took a hammer to him. X-ray shows a nondisplaced skull fracture. He's drifting in and out. Some of it's from the meds. Third curtain down."

Rook walked on back. There was a bandage on Sid's head and his face was swollen. "I could tell by your walk it was you," he said.

"Worse place they could hit you is your hard head. You ID anybody, Sid?"

"Prick cocksucker snuck me." Rosen tried to get up, but slid back down. "I got to get out of here."

"The doctor's okay, partner." He looked at the chart. "You need anything?"

Rosen tried to smile. "Nurse's name is Angela. See if she'll give me a hand job."

"Depends upon your insurance," Rook told him.

Rosen tried to smile. "Walk my dog, Lucas boy. His kidneys aren't so good."

"I'll swing by your shop. Don't go nowhere, Sid."

Dr. Ferry was coming out of a treatment room as Rook went by. "I'm going to take a look at you, Lucas, don't go anywhere. I have to remove a tennis ball from a patient's ass."

Rook rolled up on Rosen's two-story brick garage and parked his Crown Vic at an angle. He walked the perimeter slowly. He was woozy and his body hurt. Lucas leaned against the building to compose himself. Then he walked around again getting the feel of the scene.

As he was coming up on the back door, a blue and white pulled up. The cop got out, adjusting his holster and his mirrored shades, like he was some movie star. "Looking for something, friend?"

"Lose them mirrors, rookie," Lucas said.

The cop, whose name was Vance, leaned against his cruiser with his arms crossed, puffing out his biceps. "You some kind of expert? How about some expert I.D.?"

"How about I was on the job before you had your first wet dream. Call back to the house and tell them you're trying to wolf Lucas Rook."

Officer Vance took his glasses off and hung them from his shirt pocket. "Name don't mean nothing to me."

Rook shook his head. "Look, son, you call back to the precinct. You tell Big Harry you're busting my stones. See how quick you're back crossing school kids."

"You on the job?"

"Twenty happy years worth. Now, I'm going to finish my evening constitutional here. I figure I got five or six more times around the block before my bowels unclench."

"Lucas Rook, huh?" the cop said. "I'll check you out."

"You do that." Rook started back around the block. One of the street lights was out, another flickered. The 24 hour parking lot had mercury vapor lights out front. Lucas put them in the diagram in his head.

He went up the narrow alley with his maglite and his weapon leading the way. A rat the size of a cat ran out. There were metal trash cans on the right. Rook shined his light at the usual celebration of life: coffee grounds, plastic bags, dirty diapers, and pizza crusts.

He walked the perimeter again. A radiator key and a comb. Lucas put them in plastic bags and went back to the garage.

Rook ducked the scene tape and went inside. The old dog was sleeping by the desk. Nothing seemed out of order. Books everywhere. Rosen's .357 was under the mattress. The safe looked good. There was a case of Jack Daniels in the back and a TV where Sid slept. No robbery here. Lucas found two footprints in the grease and maybe a partial of a third.

He looked at his watch. Three-thirty in the morning. What a bag of shit day it had been. Rook sat down to clear his head, then walked the dog around the block like he said he would.

He went back to the St. Claire. The married cellists on the third floor were taking their cats out on leashes. Lucas nodded to the deskman, who was playing solitaire. "Black queen on the red king. He'll like that," Rook said. Old coffee room talk.

His apartment was dark, even with the lamp he left on and the two mirrors that carried its reflection. Catherine Wren had asked him more than once about why he hadn't replaced the overhead lights. They reminded him of street lights and he couldn't have the street with him 24/7. Rook heard footsteps in the hall. He took his

.45 off the mantel. Sid Rosen opened the door.

"I don't recall giving you a key, Sid."

"You didn't. One of the benefits of being a man who works with tools." He swallowed two pills. "Let me lay down. I checked myself out. I'll be out of here tomorrow. I need anything I'll just sing out." Rosen sat down on the couch. "Swell security your building got here. I tell them I'm your long lost brother, they let me in."

Rook showered while his friend slept. Then he poured a beer and went out onto the patio. The blind girl who smelled like gardenias came outside to smoke. She had sliding doors and Rook could hear them on their tracks and then the nails of her guide dog on the patio floor. He got up and started back in.

"I'm sorry," she said. "Did I interrupt your reverie?"

"I'm good," he answered.

"I hope your friend is feeling better."

Rook wondered how she knew, but offered nothing in return. "Tell him he snores like a fucking elephant," she said.

"I'll do that, Grace."

"Elegant, aren't I, Lucas?" She snubbed her cigarette out against the patio wall. "You should see me in the tub."

Sid Rosen awoke at 3 AM and turned on the light to take his meds. Rook went in to check.

"You good?"

"I'm good."

"You got to get up again, you tell me," Lucas said.

Rosen tried to arrange the pillows so that he could sleep sitting up. "Right. If I got to take a piss, you can walk me to the bathroom. These pills going to put me out for the next couple of hours. Get some sleep yourself."

Lucas opened the bathroom door a bit so he could see Sid's reflection from the living room.

"I got to take a piss, I'm not calling for an escort," Rosen said.

"You're a stubborn prick." Rook settled back on the couch. "And you snore like an elephant. My neighbor told me that and she's blind."

"You nail her yet?"

Rook turned off his light. "You're a prince, Sid."

A little after dawn, Rosen came out of the bedroom. He had his clothes on, but he wasn't walking steady. "Going to work," he said.

"In a pig's eye," Rook told him.

"Going to work."

"Not a good idea. Doc Ferry said you got to take it easy."

"You don't look so good yourself, sonny boy." Rosen leaned against the wall. "I guess I got to get my legs back." He made his way to the bedroom. "I'll go in late," he said as he lay back down.

Rook poured himself tomato juice and started on his report for Mrs. Politte's lawyers.

CHAPTER 20

Night Command meant bad jobs. The predators stalking the streets. The citizens liquored up. The shift was either hiding from their wives or messed up from their day-night rhythms being all disrupted.

Richie Haas sat at the front desk, eating candy corn, one colored section at a time. A long way from his days of running back punts in college and running down bad guys. He had just bit off another piece of yellow when Rook came in.

"Well howdy, Lucas," he said, doing his cowboy voice.

"Going up to see the Watch. How's by you?"

"Riding the range here, partner, and picking splinters from my ass."

Rook went on up.

Harry Stankey took a bite of his roast beef on rye. "Thought you'd be by," he said.

"Your p/o with the mirrored shades have something to say? He was squeezing my shoes over at Rosen's garage."

"Thinks he's Clint Eastwood, don't he? On the job thirteen months."

Lucas looked around the squad room. "Must be somebody's nephew."

"You got that right, borough councilman in Brooklyn. You here about your friend, Rosen? Nobody can fix a transmission like he can. My boy's Cougar shifted like it had swallowed the kitchen sink, but he had it running like a newborn's bowels."

"Who caught the case?"

Harry took a jar from his desk and dipped the corner of his bread into the seeded mustard. "So the way things worked out, Carmelisha and her life mate going to run it."

"You're shittin' me."

Stankey laughed and dipped his sandwich again. "It's you we're talking about. We're talking about a friend of yours, not to mention he's a good guy. Hy Gromek and Dwight Graves. Today's Graves' regular day off, so talk to Hy. Tomorrow's his RDO, so if it's tomorrow, you talk to Dwight." He saw the stains on his shirt. "Christ, first time I'm not eating with a napkin tucked in, I'm all mustarded-up. The wife's going to have to presoak this bad boy."

"How's she doing, Harry?"

"Big as a house. Must weigh two fifty. But it don't bother her, it don't bother me."

Hy Gromek came in all dressed in black. "Brother Rook," he said. "What brings you into this world of hurt?"

"Missing your face so bad, I could hardly stand it," Lucas told him. "Your goatee makes you look like a fucking movie star."

"I told you, Harry," Gromek said. "Another fine mind thinks I resemble Sean Connery."

"The garage, Hy, the case you just caught," Stankey said. "Sid Rosen. He's a friend of Rook's."

"Sure, brother Rook. We can discuss the finer points of law

enforcement while you buy me a cold beer."

Gromek grabbed a set of keys off the board and drove around to Miata's. There was no lot so they parked up the block. Gromek and Rook walked slowly, Hy because he was getting old and Rook because of his bad ribs.

"Hope we don't got to chase no evil doers, brother Rook, these patellas of mine aren't up to it."

"Appreciate the leisure pace you're taking for me, Hy. Especially you looking like a movie star the way you do."

"Thank you, Lucas," Gromek said. "Just because we live in the sewer don't mean we got to look the part."

Dobie tipped the derby he always wore. "Welcome to you, Detective, and to your fine young friend," he said.

"A pitcher for me and my uncle here," Gromek said.

They took an open booth in the rear. Gromek filled their glasses. "You want to look at the 61?"

"Something don't smell right, Hy. Nothing is boosted. Seems more like somebody had bad intentions."

Gromek nodded. "You're wise in the ways of crime, my friend." He drank. "Me too. Maybe too wise. Which is why I'm about done. Me and Dwight, we used to be the big arrest guys. Got all the major crimes, which means we got all the double time we wanted. Then they're looking at our time instead of our solve rates. Pretty soon they got us like them two little Scottie dogs, the black one and the white one on the piece of glass."

"I hear you, Hy. The job makes us question everything. Then it's questioning us. Meantime we're going to sleep in our raincoats."

Gromek poured again. "I got tired of saying 'approximately.' I got so good at making the job boring I…" He stopped short. "It's like being in a whirlpool, trying to collect the pieces of my life. I heard that somewhere. Fucked up, ain't it? Anyways, I got till the end of the month, then I'm out. Dwight, he'll be around."

The second pitcher came. "The end of the month, I'm gone,

Rook. In the meantime, I'm an inexorable mother fucker."

"Fuck 'em," Lucas said and they raised their glasses.

They went back to the 1-5, stopping along the way for Gromek to take a leak. "Got that unfinished feeling. Probably the prostrate acting up again. Got to get another ream job. Thank God my PSA keeps coming back good. Fucking doctors, all they want is to cut. You good, Rook, in the urinary department I mean?"

"I'm good. Thanks for asking."

A black dog lifted its leg across the street.

"Good to see you, Hy," Rook said. "I'll check in with your partner tomorrow."

"Dwight and me don't talk on our days off, Rook, unless it's something hot or somebody's jamming us up, the way the politics does. It has kept us a happy couple for nine years." They shook hands. "DG is almost as old as me, but he's still got the smeller. Can find the bad guy from his dinner table." Gromek adjusted his hat as they went up the bank steps. "He looks like Bill Cosby," he said, then hurried his pace to take another piss.

Lucas decided to stop back at Miata's. Best thing was if he sat at the bar. The bartender would remember him, and maybe he could get something off of that.

There were two stools open. One was in front of the door. Rook took the one next to a red-faced man smoking one cigarette after another. The smoker went over to the cigarette machine. He rocked it hard. "Three fifty for smokes, Dobie? You turning kike on me?"

The bartender shook his head.

Eddie Gaul went back to his stool and relit a butt. "Fuck you, then. I'll get 'em up the road."

"I ain't emptying your ashtrays no more tonight," Dobie said. "Finish your VO and water. You're flagged."

"Fuck you twice then. And your sister." He downed his drink and got up to leave, colliding with a couple coming in. Eddie gave them a shove. The woman shoved him back. He saw who it was and went on out.

A well-dressed black man in his fifties came in, wearing a navy blue suit and a gray turtleneck. "First smart thing he did all night," he said.

"You got that right," Dobie told him. "Andi, she'd have knocked him out for sure."

"No shit," Lucas said.

"No shit," the bartender said. He poured a shot of Crown Royal.

"On me," Rook said.

"Thank you, kind sir."

"You partnered up with Hy?" Rook asked.

Dwight Graves waited for him to go on.

"Told me you were an older gentleman, looked like Bill Cosby's father, Hy did."

"Who's that?"

"My uncle Hy from the 1-5, sporting that new face hair."

Graves sipped his drink. "Right. And he's Robert Culp."

"Shrimp in the basket, Dobie," Rook said. "Going to see a man about a horse."

When Lucas went back to the men's room, the bartender leaned over. "He came in with your partner. He had a pitcher in the back. Looks familiar."

"That's Lucas Rook," Graves said. "Took out the pukes that did his brother. Used to be on the job, both of them, him and Kirk."

"Right," Dobie said. "He offed the pricks they shot his twin brother. I remember, in front of the Sephora Club. He walks like a cop even gimped up."

Lucas Rook came back.

"The back says we're out of shrimp. Roast pork's good."

Rook picked up the menu.

"You searching for something, my friend?" Dwight asked.

"Roast pork's good if you got a Kaiser roll, Dobie. Mustard and onion. Otherwise, the chili. No cheese." He swiveled on his stool.

"Your partner tells me they got your RDO's so he wouldn't be talking to you for a couple of days. It can wait."

Graves smiled and extended his hand. "Lucas Rook, right. I knew your brother, over at the 7th. Good cop." He lifted his drink. "*Fidelis ad mortem*," he said. "Kirk and me worked this case together. Grabbed up this Shanti Ashmead trying to hid out in all these Hasids. Black hat and all. Except his afro didn't have no curls." He shook his head, laughing.

Rook finished his beer. "You caught this case, a friend of mine. Took a beating in his spot on Gansevont Street."

Graves nodded. "Right. Garage. He's some kind of mechanical genius, right. Me, I lease them. They need fixing, I let the dealer do it."

"Friend of mine, Sid Rosen."

Dwight finished his drink. "You got a number I can reach you at?"

Rook handed over one of his cards. They shook hands.

"Your brother was a good cop," Graves said. "The pricks got what they deserved."

CHAPTER 21

The cab driver toasted Rook with his can of grape soda. "Never forget a face," he said. "I'm shit with names though." He took a swig. "I got to swing around and drop a deuce. Super over on 56th lets me use the john. Then I'll swing back if everything goes okay."

"You're giving me way too much information, Bobby Haak. Way too much."

Lucas hailed another cab. "Your destination, sir?" the driver asked. She was a stunning woman with a Haitian lilt in her voice.

"166 Fifth," Rook told her.

She nodded and continued with the conversation on her headset. When they pulled up in front of his office building, Rook paid the fare and gave her another five. "I'm going up to get my mail. Be here when I get down." She nodded.

Lucas swiped his card and went inside his building. The vestibule was cold and only one elevator was running. Rook heard rattling from the fire door and turned to face it with his hand on his gun butt.

"Building's closed," the super said. "We don't open for an hour and a half."

Lucas pushed the elevator button. "You look swell in those slippers."

The super saw who it was and let the remark pass. Rook had helped his nephew out with a GTA last year.

There was mail sticking out from his letter slot and a mailing tube from Attorney Gavilan, Lucy and Ricky from sunny Florida. The light was on next door. Rook had seen the photographer only once since he first moved in two years ago. Thin man with a blank face.

The mail was the usual. Another tax bill, a reminder from his accountant, a brochure from the Oceanaire Motel to "come again," an invitation to a reunion at Antopol's place in Garden City.

The answering machine flashed. He got rid of the answering service when Phelps told him that messages his clients left with the service were discoverable in criminal and civil litigation. Attorney Eck calling for an update, a potential client looking for his sister, and a hang-up. Then Dr. Mesoros. "This is Jaimie Mesoros. I'm going to be in Manhattan. I'll call back."

She had something on her mind. Hopefully, it involved the body fluids. Things were slow since Catherine Wren got a bug up her ass. Rook moved the *Post* and *Shotgun News* from his desk. With a little more clean-up, he found a calendar. Today said, "Tuzio."

When he got back downstairs the taxi was gone. Another cabbie saw him and angled over. The Haitian driver cut him out. "He's my fare, mon. Still on my meter, mon."

Lucas got in. She was still talking to whoever on the headset. At the St. Claire she tried to double-charge him for the waiting time. He shook his head and went inside. Nobody was at the front desk. He went upstairs.

The phone rang as Lucas opened the door. A call from Kirk's wife, Ann. He let the machine pick it up. She had re-married and one of her stepsons always got into the shit. Rook had seen her at a wedding three years ago. She had a smile on her face, but her eyes were still a widow's. He was sorry that he had seen her at all.

Lucas hung his pants over the bedroom door and put on a pair of sweats. He went over what he knew about Sid's case, working the grid from his years on the job.

He lay down and drifted in and out of sleep. The phone rang. "My wife also says I snore like a fucking elephant," Sid said. "I said thank you, dear. I'll be back at the garage tomorrow. You grab the scumbag yet? Hold him for me."

"It's me, Sid."

"I thought I had gotten your machine, Lucas."

"You good?"

"I'm good. A little confused is all. Doctor said I'll have that a little."

Rook scratched at the scar on his leg. "You want me to walk that old fleabag for you?"

"I got him out here, on the Island. The wife, she treats him like a baby. But no way it's permanent. She'll have him in a bra and panties."

"I'm here, partner," Rook said and hung up. He looked at the clock although he knew what time it was. He always did, whether he was awake or not.

Lucas took a shower and went over to Joe Oren's for breakfast. After, he'd work some more on his report, see Tuzio, call back Mrs. Politte's lawyer. Then maybe see Dr. Mesoros, who smelled like lemons.

Joe came in with a crate of eggs. "Fucking deliveries get later and later. Wholesaler tries to hang it on 9-11. I said they holding all these eggs up to see Bin Laden's inside? Prick says they could be. Knows no way I'm driving down to Vineland like the old days."

"You need anything done?"

"He gave me five pounds of butter and a gallon of chocolate

milk on the house."

"So it's okay?"

"Eggs-actly," Oren said.

Joe poured Rook a cup of coffee. "Shorthanded again, Lucas. Sam's day off. You know anybody reliable, I'm looking. The other girls did their part, and it's stretching it for Jeanie to come in with her classes and all. She's going to be a teacher, you know."

Jeanie came out of the kitchen. "I heard your voice, Lucas Rook. I made you a mushroom omelet, fluffy the way you like it."

"Fluffy?" Joe Oren asked. "I didn't think you'd like anything that was 'fluffy.'"

"That's not right, Daddy."

"That is not right, Daddy," Lucas said. "Rye toast, Jeanie girl."

"It's in," she said and went over to take a new customer's order.

The man got up and went to the men's room. Jeanie came back with the toast. "Do you think I'm fat, Lucas Rook? Daddy says I'm getting fat."

"I did not," Joe said.

"Well, I am. I'm getting fat."

"You're not fat, Jeanie girl. You're…"

"You're fine, Jeanie," Joe Oren said. "You take after your mother."

"I'll get real skinny, go on a diet. Lucas Rook and I are getting married, Daddy."

Lucas shook his head. He finished his second cup of coffee and read part of the paper.

"You got donuts, Joe? Going to see Tuzio."

"A couple. Let me throw in some Danish."

Rook paid his bill and gave Jeanie's hand a little squeeze. "I'd be honored to marry you, Jeanie girl. And you are not fat."

"Wait till you see me, Lucas Rook. I'll get so skinny. They'll have to paint my jeans on."

"You're just fine," Lucas said.

He left to see Tuzio.

The second Tuesday of the month, Rook went to the Policeman's Home. Ray Tuzio was his last partner. Now the diabetes had got him bad and they were cutting him up, piece by piece. "Don't let them take my pink toes," Ray said over and over with one leg gone altogether and the other up to the knee. Sometimes he made sense and sometimes he didn't. He had started to piss himself.

Today was not a good day. As Rook came in, he heard Ray Tuzio yelling, "On the gate. On the gate," that they should let him out while someone else stayed locked away.

"You okay, brother?" Lucas asked him.

Tuzio drifted off, then came around. "I got to do them 5's," he said. "Can't type at all, my hands too big for them little keys." He tried to get out of bed but couldn't.

Jim McGloan walked in and sat on the other bed. He had worn real thin. "Time's the baddest perpetrator of them all," he said.

Rook got up. His partner was sleeping. "Look after Tuze, will ya Jim."

"I'll do that, boy-o," said McGloan and he too went into sleep.

Lucas Rook drove away remembering the day he brought Ray Tuzio to the home. "Let me hold those aviators, Tuze. There's no glare in here, partner." The nurse or social worker or whatever kept calling him "Mr. Torio" for some reason, but let Ray hold his sunglasses, which they couldn't get from him anyway.

The crime scene tape was back up when Rook returned the Crown Vic to Sid Rosen's garage. He flashed the remote and the garage door opened. Sid sat behind the desk with his eyes closed.

"What you doing here?" Lucas asked him.

"Reading."

"Sure, Sid."

"Absorbing some Dickens here, son. Knew if I stayed home, I'd have to shoot her."

"Probably not a good idea." Lucas hung the keys up on the board. "You put the scene tape back up, Sid?"

"Give me a little peace and quiet. Catch up on my backlog. Customers'll have to wait a couple more days." He rubbed his eyes.

"Take it easy, partner," Rook said.

"You get anything on them assholes who assailed me, Lucas? You grab them up for me. I got some getting even to do."

"There more than one, Sid? PD thinks there's one."

"Don't know, Rook. Right now I'm seeing two of everything. You talking right now, I'm seeing two of you."

"That's not a good thing, Sid."

Rosen put his head down as Lucas left.

CHAPTER 22

Ben and Carmen's was down on Carmine Street. Rook went there to get a haircut and tell Carmen how his brother was doing.

Carmen Tuzio ran his hand over his own bald head. "Little off the top. Give you the Carmen special."

Rook got in the chair with some difficulty.

"You look like a freight train hit you, Lucio."

"He did. Little off the top like always. Leave the back long."

Carmen took a pair of scissors from the blue antiseptic. "Been cutting your hair since you was a kid. And your brother's too, God rest his soul."

Lucas closed his eyes. "I saw Ray. He's doing okay."

"Shave on the house, Lucio," Carmen said. He tilted the chair back. The hot lather felt good, the razor going across Rook's face and neck. Then the hot and cold towels and a splash of Lilac Vegetal.

"Like a new man," Carmen said as he set the chair back up.

"It's good," Lucas told him. He tipped to cover part of the shave and then went into the back to take a piss. There was still some blood in his urine. The ribs would be tender for another couple of weeks, which meant he'd better not be starting anything unless he could finish it fast.

When Rook came back out there was a fat man in the chair and another waiting with his face behind a newspaper. Lucas didn't like the way that looked.

"You got my paper, there, chief," Rook told him.

The man had a thick accent. "I'm sorry," he said.

"No problem. I read it anyway." Being paranoid was a protective thing, like the way some animals turned white in the winter. Acting on it was only wrong when it got in the way.

Rook went to his office to complete his report. Then he'd call Mrs. Politte's lawyer back, which would give him more billing.

Both elevators were running for a change. The Korean got in one, the Japanese in the other. Mrs. McCormick, who wore a scarf to hide her goiter, said good morning.

The mailman got on at two to ride up a floor. They'd have a chat about him not pushing the mail through the slot.

Another call on his machine from Dr. Mesoros. This time she lost the "Jaimie." "I do need to see you. As I'm going to be in Manhattan this afternoon, I'm going to take the liberty of stopping at your office."

There goes romance. He'd have to straighten up the place. Lucas looked at the clock. Time to finish the report and make his call before he got domestic.

Lucas had six pages of notes on his narrow reporter's pad. They were in a code of police abbreviations and his own language of geometric symbols and shorthand. It gave him four pages of double-spaced text without the details of his run-in with Jack Curran, Big Earl and Turkey Neck. "Uncooperative persons" was enough for this report. People in business rarely liked to be informed that their employees were getting into fights. He referenced the need for on-going investigation, including a background and investigation of the sex harasser, spicy enough to keep the job going a couple of extra days. He also mentioned the consultation with the funeral home, which he intended to be by phone.

Rook stamped "Attorney-Client Privileged Work Product" on each page like Phelps had told him and would call Eck before he sent the reply out. They were looking for something specific or wanted something omitted, he would help them if he could. The old adage, "he who controls the checkbook, controls the game" went a long way in his business.

Mail came halfway through the slot as the phone rang. "Hold, please," he said as he got up to go for the mailman. Moving was difficult because of the guarding he was doing for his ribs and his bad leg. Together they were starting to get to his low back. By the time Lucas got to the door, the letter carrier had delivered to the hermit next door and was preparing to hijack the elevator so he wouldn't have to walk a flight.

"Hey, postal," he called. "We need to have a chat."

"Speedy Delivery," said the mailman. "Speedy Delivery," he said as the elevator doors opened and closed.

Rook remembered the call on hold. Felix Gavilan asking if he got the lovely calendar and to keep him in mind if he came across unrepresented defendants. "I'm sure I'll need your services on each one of those cases," the lawyer said.

"I'll keep you in mind, Felix. It goes both ways. I got you right here on my Rolodex."

"Mil gracias, Mr. Rook."

"De nada," Lucas said and he hung up.

He looked at the clock. Time to get a shoeshine and a meatball sandwich before the lovely doctor was to arrive.

"Hop on up, Mr. Rook," Jimbo Turner said. "Your leg must be

acting out the way you're walking. You come clippety-cloppety down my street like that Chester fella from *Gunsmoke*."

"How's it been, Jimbo?"

"Not bad for a diabetic old white shineman." He ran his fingers across Rook's shoes. "Seems you've been out and about. You bring that sweet corn, Mr. Rook?"

"Haven't got to Jersey yet, but when I do, I'll bring you back a bagful. And some beefsteak tomatoes if they look good."

Jimbo rolled up Rook's pants cuffs. "Nothin' better than a thick slice of good tomato, slice of onion and some salt and pepper. Makes a sandwich so's a poor man's like a king."

"Anything on the street?"

"Same old same old." He rubbed polish in with his fingertips. "I appreciate you taking care of that thing for me, street bum pissin' in my phone booth the way he was. Seems like no place's free from sacrilege. Like your friend Sid's place got took down. That's not right."

"Any caper go down you're not aware of, Jimbo Turner?"

"Something touches my world, Lucas, I feel it. You doing fine, my friend?"

"I'm good."

The shineman clicked the brushes together. "You been throwing shots with your ankle piece. I can smell it good."

"Out at the range. Didn't have time to clean it."

"Yes, sir, Mr. Rook." He kept his head down and worked the shoes so they shone like glass.

The line at Checchia's was long, but when the owner saw Rook, he called him over.

"Meatball to go," Rook said.

Somebody from the line said something, but Mrs. C, who was working the grille, told them to stuff themselves. Rook took his sandwich and a Dr. Brown's black cherry and went back up to his office. He ate fast, but like a king.

If he wasn't expecting Jaimie Mesoros, he might not have recognized her at all. Her black hair was down. Her unbuttoned leather coat showed a slit skirt, high boots, and fine legs. Expert makeup highlighted her eyes and mouth.

"I'm sorry, I should have knocked."

"That's good. I was just starting…" He moved some things around. "To straighten up."

"I'm sorry I interrupted your lunch."

"Dinner, really."

"Well, there goes that idea. I wanted to buy you dinner." She took off her coat. "I thought we could have something to eat, have some wine, talk."

"You know what I do for a living?"

"It says so on your door, Lucas Rook."

"I just want to know if I'm supposed to call you 'Doctor' and whether to change my shirt."

"Jaimie is fine." She pushed her dark hair away from her face.

Lucas got up. "There's a Chinese restaurant a block over. They'll have bean curd, whatever."

"Lead the way, kind sir."

Rook had pork fried rice there once or twice a week. The owner, whose name was Tommy, was glad to see him. "How are you doing today, Lucas McCain? And your lovely friend?" He took them to a table in the rear.

"McCain?" Jaimie asked him.

"Lucas McCain from *The Rifleman*, a TV show with Chuck Connors. Tommy is quite the movie buff."

"Chuck Connors was one of the few to play both pro basketball and baseball like Conley, Sanders. I think there were some more. My dad's quite a baseball nut."

Rook poured the tea.

"I didn't figure you for a tofu fan, Lucas Rook."

"I'm not unless it's wrapped around a lamb chop."

They ate and had a Tsing Tao each. Not enough alcohol to get them anywhere.

Jaimie Mesoros put her arm through Rook's as they walked back. "It's nice," she said.

Lucas stopped outside his office building. "You have something to talk to me about, Dr. Mesoros, or is it my big blue eyes?"

"I don't want to go home, Lucas Rook. Not tonight."

"Is there something else you have to tell me, Jaimie?"

"Not tonight," she said. "Tonight is just for us."

They went to his room, where the only light was from the other buildings in the night. She came to him and they breathed each other's breath. "I wish the world would go away," she said, "and leave us just like this."

CHAPTER 23

Jumpy Ames had his nose in a pair of size 10's when Lucas Rook came up on him.

"Still at it, Jumpy?"

Ames jerked his head up and dropped the shoe. "No, it's not like that."

Lucas slipped in behind him. "Still jumpy, aren't we? You got something to hide, Jumpy Ames?"

"Christ, Detective. You know it's not like that." He sprayed the inside of the shoe and put it with the others. "You just stopping by or you want to roll a few?"

"Right, Jumpy. Bowling's my favorite pastime." He picked up one of the rental shoes. "Watching the ball roll down and come back again makes me all goofy, like from sniffing other people's sweaty feet."

Two teams came up. One dressed in purple. The other in green.

Ames set them up. "You gentlemen ready?" he asked.

"Ready to rumble," said one of the purple in horn-rimmed glasses.

"You got that right," said the leader of the green.

Lucas waited until the bowlers were gone, then dropped a ball on Jumpy's foot.

Ames hopped up and down. "Jesus Christ, Rook, you breaked my big toe."

"It was only one of those eight-pounders. I wanted to break your foot, I wouldn't use one of them kiddie's balls. I'll use the regulation one next time."

Ames took his shoe off and rubbed his foot. Rook picked up the shoe and shoved it in Jumpy's face. "What you call this when you do your own?"

The phone rang.

"Leave it be," Lucas said.

"I can't. Maybe it's a pizza party or something. We got leagues starting up and all."

Rook grabbed Jumpy's little finger and bent it back. "You're wasting my time, 'shoe boy.' Let's take a little walk."

Ames winced from the pain. "I only got one shoe on," he said.

"Playing hard to get, Jumpy. You're such a tease. Now lead the way."

They went back to the storage room. It was filled with boxes of janitorial supplies and plastic jugs.

"I ain't done nothing wrong, Lucas Rook."

"Didn't say you did." He pushed the door closed with one hand and Jumpy down with the other. Then he took Ames' glasses.

"You want my size elevens up close and personal?"

"It ain't like that. You know it, Detective."

"I meant on your little rat face." He waved the glasses back and forth. "Didn't want to break these here. You know they might not be in your health plan."

Jumpy Ames covered up. "This ain't right."

"It is right because you're a low-rent con who goes away again, you're not coming back. Unless you like that, with all them prison shoes to huff."

"I ain't…"

Rook put the glasses down and took off his jacket. "You know what happens next."

Jumpy tried to get away. Rook pulled him back. "Know you a long time. I pinched you more than once and let you walk a couple of times. Going to ask you two questions, Jumpy. Don't shit me because your face depends on it. One, who did the crimes at Sid Rosen's garage? Who took a hammer to him? Two, you don't know, you tell me when you'll know. Now, I'm going to count to three, then I'm going to tune you up real bad. I'm going to make a mess of things."

Ames was shaking. "Don't know, Detective. Don't know. Let me be. I'll find out. Always done good for you, haven't I? Heard about the caper on my scanner is all."

"Don't shit me, Jumpy, not even a little bit."

"For true, for true. That's all I got, Lucas Rook. Heard it on my scanner's all. You need me on this. Always been true, ain't I?"

"Don't push it, shitbird. You heard it on your scanner?"

"On the police band, Lucas Rook. Howie still paying a C-note for his wreckers."

"Another C-note in it for you to do good, Jumpy, and I don't crack you."

Ames relaxed. "Okay, Detective, okay."

Lucas Rook walked in close. "You give me who did it. You get into your network of scum and thieves. You get to me real soon."

"Always been right with you, Detective Rook. Since you gave me rhythm that time when my mom was sick."

Rook grabbed him by the throat. "No rhythm on this, Mr. Ames. No rhythm at all."

Lucas went back outside and went over to the Stroll. A hot dog cart was at the corner, supplying light refreshment for the whores. The vendor was somebody he had seen before. "I know you," Rook said.

"Maybe my brother," the vendor said.

"Maybe."

A telephone repairman walked up. "How's it going, George?" he said.

"I'll remember where I saw you, Georgie-Boy," Lucas said. "Count on it."

The parade was going on like always at the Stroll. The old timers. New faces already old. You could tell by the way they walked how long they been in the life. The new ones working it too hard, the old timers not caring they were pieces of garbage. More white faces, the Russians moving in. Half of them looking like Britney Spears, the other half like Bela Lugosi.

Big Leon started over to Rook. He was six foot five and wearing a thong. Amy pulled him away. "He wants a date, girl, you tell him to buy a calendar."

"Thank you, Miss Amy," Leon said as he wiggled away.

"How's by you?" Rook said.

"Business is business. Besides, I never saw a prick I didn't like. What you doing over here? You ready to fall in love?"

Shavon walked up looking like Halle Berry. "Creamy rich," she said.

"Right," Amy said. "If he don't mind a pair of hairy balls. Now run along, girl."

"Then tell your hunk of a friend not to be eating me up with his eyes," Shavon said as she went on down the line.

A silver BMW slid up to the curb. Crystal Lee went over with skin as white as snow.

"Looking for who beat Sid Rosen, Amy."

"That nice man. I used to send him house calls. He was partial to Crystal Lee. Not the one just rode off, the one whose name she took. The HIV? You got to watch that shit."

"You taking care, Amy?"

"Me, I'd double bag the Pope. You tell Sid when he's feeling better, that Crystal Lee just died. Meanwhile, you let me hold both ends of a Ulysses Grant, I'll see you're done right. The stock market had not gone into the toilet, I'd be gone to my house in Maine. Meanwhile I know this stroll like King Solomon knew his diamond mines. I hear all kinds of things when the men got their pants off."

"Deal," Lucas said. He gave her the fifty and swung away. Rook had his route, and he would make the rest of his stops before swinging by The Stroll again. When his spadework was done, he'd check back in at the precinct.

Shirl Freleng ran the newsstand at Broadway and 23rd. She had been running it since her father died. Shirl was there from when the papers got thrown off the truck a little after 5 AM until a little before 6 at night.

From 2 to 2:30, she pulled her racks of magazines and mints inside and closed the shutters and her eyes. She took her shoes off and put her feet up. Pity be the one who rapped on her stand when she did.

Rook rolled up just as Shirl was opening back up again. She nodded and shook his hand. She wore work gloves with the fingers cut out.

"Still wearing your pearl handle up under your vest?" he asked her.

"You enforcing that Sullivan Law?" She poured them each a cup of coffee from her thermos. "No way in hell I ever pay four dollars for a coffee."

"Sid Rosen got roughed up," Rook said.

"I heard that," Shirl said as she refilled her cup.

"Where'd you hear that, Shirl?" Lucas showed a twenty.

A wide man in a leather coat came up for the racing forms.

"Feeling lucky," he said.

"Len Oser. Unluckiest man in the world. Loses everything, hair, family, job, but keeps at it. L-Oser. 'Loser,' get it?"

Rook put the twenty away. "How'd you hear, Shirl?"

"Nothing romantic, Rook. Got a customer rides the sector car."

"The goof with the mirrored shades?"

"Not that clown. Know him though. Tried to work me a couple of times. I says you're supposed to be checking I'm okay when I'm opening up, not hitting me up for magazines and whatnot." She straightened a stack of newspapers. "Sid okay?"

"He's good." Lucas took a *Newsweek* and put down the twenty.

"Didn't know you were a reader, Lucas Rook."

"Got to keep my waiting room up-to-date for my high-class clientele, Shirl. You get anything, call me."

"Television, telegram, tell a woman. You know how it is."

Rook picked up a couple of packs of her cigarettes. "Stamps are pretty good, Shirl, but selling bootleg smokes can get you jammed up pretty good."

"I'll keep that in mind," she said. "I'll keep that in mind."

Wingy Rosenzweig lived on the top floor of a brownstone in the Park Slope section of Brooklyn compliments of his late wife, who had the good sense to be born rich, and the bad luck to have an aneurism. Along the way, Wingy had done quite nicely himself, buying and selling out-of-date pharmaceuticals.

Lucas stopped at the corner deli for pastrami sandwiches, and Wingy was glad to see him. "How ya doing, Lucas, boy? How's that Princeton girl?"

"She threw me out, Wingy. She couldn't stand my something or other."

Rosenzweig adjusted the photo on his end table, a beautiful blonde woman with her hand on Wingy's good arm and him waving at the camera with his flipper arm. The two of them wearing

Hawaiian shirts and smiling like they just invented ice cream.

"The hardest part isn't saying goodbye, Lucas boy. It's not saying hello again. Did I just say that?" He opened a beer. "It's poetry or whatever."

The doorbell rang. Rosenzweig buzzed them up and answered his door. "Where's Eddie?" he asked the delivery boy.

"I don't know. I'm just delivering this Chinese food. I don't know nothing about whoever."

"Keep the change," Wingy said, "of which there's not going to be none since you're a rude prick."

Lucas and Rosenzweig ate in front of the television, pastrami sandwiches and Chinese food. "Going blind, Lucas Rook. Got this macular degeneration, putting holes in my eyes." He turned to look over his shoulder at the picture of him and his wife. "Last thing I see is her smiling, I'm alright. But you didn't come to pay your friend Wingy a visit. Except you looking to cop some meds, which I don't deal in any more, as you know."

The hot and sour soup made Rook's nose run. "Some puke got my friend Sid. Worked him over with a ball peen hammer."

"So you figured I'd have something for you?"

"Now or later."

Rosenzweig took a bite of his sandwich and twirled some lo mein. "Sooner or later. Except I'll work that it's sooner."

Rook finished his meal and went back to The Stroll. Should have asked Wingy for some out-of-date Zantac.

Bambi Cabresa was parked up on the curb in his white Escalade with the big gold rims. He waved a chalky girl over. "You name's Pinky now. So don't be calling yourself Loretta or whatever."

"Pinky," she said.

"Let me see you work," he said and he offered up one of the buttons on his mink full length. She sucked on it like a kitten on a teat. "Now go out there, girl, and suck it good. Next time I see you, I might change your name again."

Shavon came up to Rook, whirling and twirling in a sequined coat. "Ms. Amy told me to say she had to take her little one to get his ears checked, I'm to tell you."

"Thanks, Shavon. She have anything else to say?"

"Only that I shouldn't be bothering you and that I should be a good girl cause you're probably only playing hard to get."

Stosh Gromek sat at his round kitchen table in his dress blue uniform and a pajama top.

"You don't have to pull parade duty anymore, Pop," Hy said.

Lucille Fontana from next door came in with a pot of soup. "Things I remember most about growing up is the salt air and soup," she said.

"We were out here before the bridges came," Stosh said to no one in particular.

The phone rang. Detective Gromek picked it up. "We got the perp on the garage job," his partner told him.

Hy stretched the phone cord back to the table so he could get at the piece of meat in his soup.

"Stanwyck's the apprehending," Graves went on. "The clearance is ours. Some scum snatches this old lady's purse, which leads to his being pinched and promptly educated about the Flash Stanwyck Examination Procedure and how penetrating that's going to be. Persuasive as he is, Stanwyck puts his flashlights away and the puke takes him to this alley in which is found the old lady's purse and to everyone's surprise, our garage job perpetrator, who happens to be deceased."

"The collar do him?"

"Flash says the poor bastard tossed his cookies when he sees the stiff."

Gromek speared another piece of meat. "The DOA?"

"Plays out he's the fine citizen who did Rosen."

"Talk to me, Dwight."

Graves relit his cigar. "The scene reads like a text book. Perp falls off a fire escape trying to make another illegal entry. He got motor oil on the bottoms of his shoes, and got a ball peen hammer on him got blood on it."

"That's our boy. We should run a check, see if we can clear some other cases with the same M.O." Hy looked at his watch. "I get in the next hour, it gives me a comp day. And maybe we should have a chat with Lucas Rook. Make sure there's no loose ends."

"Maybe we shouldn't bet too complicated, Hy. You can reach out and touch that retirement."

"Maybe," Hy said.

Stosh Gromek got up from the table. "I've got rice pudding," Lucille told him.

His father went down the hall. "We was all walking on the beach," he said.

Hy shook his head. "I appreciate your help, Lucille. I really do."

"That's what friends are for," she said. Lucille looked out the window as she spoke.

When Hy Gromek got back to the squad, Dwight Graves and Detective Crowder were the only two there. Crowder was on her way out. "Chief of D's got a raccoon up his ass," Andi said as she left.

Gromek moved his name over on the board. "Let's grab a decent cup of coffee," he said.

Iannarelli came in with a bowling bag in each hand. "Got a head in each one," he offered as Dwight and Hy walked by.

Graves had managed one of the new SUV's that came into the squad. "Man says he's going to invent a car, rides like shit, tips in a heartbeat, guzzles gas like a swine, you tell him he's crazy."

"You pulled it, partner."

Graves took an angled turn. "It makes me feel suburban, Hy. It surely does."

They went over to Miata's. Dobie was behind the bar. "Starsky and Hutch," he said as they came in. The two detectives took their usual seat in the last booth.

"I tried you over at the house first, Hy," Graves said. "Pauline said you're at your Pop's."

"Appreciate it, partner. Anyways, he's talking about taking the dog for a walk. Buddy's been buried out back for ten years." Their coffee came. "Christ, Dwight, that dog used to chase chickens up and down the road. Can you imagine that? Now it's all developments and so on, and they're getting old. He tells me we start talking about a nursing home he swallows his gun, which I took out of the house months ago." Hy used his napkin to wipe off an imaginary spot. "You're thinking I'm thinking Rook did the puke in the dumpster?"

"It's messy, but could be." Dwight took out a cigar, but didn't light it.

Dobie brought their coffees and a piece of cheesecake with two forks. Gromek looked at his watch. "I called Rook. Said it was about the garage job. He said he'd meet me here."

Lucas came in, walking stiff from the beating he took. "It's nice to see seniors dating," he said.

"Can't get anything by a trained detective," Hy told him.

"Two forks, one plate's a giveaway. What you got, gents?"

"The puke did your buddy, got a sheet as long as Wilt Chamberlain's jimmy," Graves said.

"He cop to it?" Rook asked.

"Not hardly."

Dobie came over with coffee for Lucas and refilled the other two cups. "Another piece of cheesecake, gentlemen?"

"You twisted my arm," Hy Gromek said.

"Make that two," Lucas said. "Unless you got pie, apple or whatever." He sipped his coffee. "So you got the perp…"

"The perp's DOA, Lucas," Hy told him.

"You gents going to start the band playing or do you want me to?" Rook said.

"Meaning what?" Graves asked.

Rook stirred his coffee in one direction and then the other. "Meaning I'm seeing two Scottie dogs dancing on that glass."

"You figure we're trying to jam you up?" Hy asked. "That's not right."

Dobie came over with the desserts, but Gromek waved him by.

"At least to sniff my ass," Rook said.

"That's not right and you know it," Dwight Graves told him. "No way we do you like that."

"Excuse me, I'm a cynical prick, gentlemen. I see <u>two</u> fine detectives talking to somebody, I figure…"

Graves stood up. "You got this, Hy?" he said. "I'll be back in a while. Miata's don't let you smoke here no more, and I got this three-dollar Honduran calling me."

Gromek let him go and started in on his cheesecake. "You're a paranoid cynical prick, Lucas. But I don't blame you. We both've seen more than one man good enough to be the first one through the door, be the first one they hang out to dry." He put his fork down. "I figure the scumbag tuned your friend, he's up a fire escape. He falls. He dies. Our case is cleared. I thought you'd want to know."

"And to see my face when you told me," Rook said. He took a

forkful of Hy's cake. "Tell me about the perp."

"The jitbag's name is Suder. Petty thief. Did time upstate off of some smash and grabs. We ran him off his prints and his jailhouse tat. Got a half circle branded on him fresh. He mean anything to you?"

Rook sipped his coffee. "He don't. We got anything else here?"

"Nothing on my plate but a half a piece of cheesecake."

"That's good," Rook said.

He left two dollars on the table and another on the bar. Maybe yes and maybe no Hy and his partner were running something on him. If they were just updating him or even if they had done him a favor or whatever, they both wouldn't have been there. Gromek was a good guy, but Lucas knew a lot of things changed when retirement was getting close.

In any case, no way was that half-circle brand a coincidence. Lucas Rook took a deep breath and reminded himself to pay attention to billing Mrs. Politte while he did what needed doing. He was going to pay Turkey Neck and Big Earl a visit that they never would forget.

CH**A**PTER

Rook looked at his watch when he got out to the parking lot. Jumpy Ames would be hard at work sniffing a parade of bowling shoes. Amy would be hard at work with her head in some commuter's lap. He could call Wingy. Shirl would have to wait until morning. He'd check the shoe shine stand as he left town.

The bowling alley was jammed with pastors, postal workers, and pharmacists in garish shirts. An ugly woman was at the counter making change.

"I don't know 'Jumpy' Ames, Mister," she said with gapped teeth. "But my manager's name is Ames, and he is on vacation. My employees get paid vacation and he's earned it."

Lucas wanted to tell her that her mouth looked like a 7-10 split, but he let it go. "Well, you tell him that Lucas Rook stopped by. I'm sure he'll be sorry we missed each other."

Two men came over to argue about the foul light on lane 16, and the chubby Kingpins came in early for their showdown. Lucas took a piss and made another pass at The Stroll.

Miss Amy was just getting out of a black Lexus coupe. Her platinum wig was askew.

"You okay, girl?" Rook asked.

She straightened herself up. "Going to need a trip to my chiropractor the way my client subluxed my cervical vertebrae."

"Hazards of the trade."

"Without no worker's comp. Still got my ear to the street for you. That nice man okay yet? Seems he was a client of mine sometime back. House calls as I recall. He was partial to Crystal Lee, who just died of a broken heart."

A white Bentley flashed its lights a half block down. "Basketball players in town," she said and started her business walk down the street. "Girl gotta eat," she said. "You take care. Give my hello to Mr. Sid."

Lucas Rook went back to the St. Claire. He needed the rest, and his friends upstate could wait another half a day before he paid them a visit. Jaimie Mesoros was not in his apartment, but the place still smelled like her. Lucas made himself a grilled cheese and drank a Miller Lite. His ribs still hurt and his kidneys, but that was it for the codeine. He wanted to be clear-headed when he brought his revenge to Oneonta.

Rook checked his messages at home and at the office. A hang-up on each and another automated call to tell him he had won a free trip to Disneyland. Jaimie Mesoros had called each place and left a message that she was at her father's and it was important. She'd call back.

Lucas called Wingy, who picked up on the first ring. "Well, Detective Rook, I guess that is that, unless you're calling to inquire about my health. I'm going blind, you know."

"What's what, Wingy?"

"What's what is that's that. They found what you're looking for."

"Talk to me, Wingy."

"In the dumpster, Lucas Rook. In the dumpster. I still have customers work in law enforcement. You need anything, you not feeling good, you call up Wingy. I'll take care of you."

Lucas ran the tub and took some Advils. As he was getting in to soak, the phone rang again. It was Jaimie. "I need you, Lucas Rook," she said.

"What's up?"

"It's my father. He's in trouble, Lucas. I need you."

"I'm halfway in the tub, Jaimie. I'll call you back in twenty minutes unless he's in physical danger."

"You just can't fuck me and forget me, Lucas."

"I just can't fuck you *twice* and forget you, Jaimie. I'll call you back like I said I would. I'm getting in the tub before the water gets cold."

Rook lowered himself into the bath wondering whether the fucking he got wouldn't be worth the fucking he'd get. The hot water felt good, and he stretched out his bad leg on the end of the tub. He should have remembered to put Epsom salts in. Some of the old remedies still worked.

As he was toweling off, the phone rang again. "You said fifteen minutes. It's been twenty-five," Jaimie said.

Lucas put the phone on hands-free and grabbed a pair of jockey shorts. "Take a chill pill, Doc. I'm standing here balls naked. Fine balls at that, I remember you saying."

"My father's in trouble. I told you that."

He put on a pair of sweat pants and a pullover. "You did, Jaimie. You just didn't tell me what kind of trouble you're talking about."

"He said we shouldn't talk over the phone."

Rook picked the receiver up. "Is he in danger, Jaimie? Is somebody trying to hurt him physically? Are you in danger?"

"I need to see you."

"Jaimie, I don't know what's going on. If you want me to talk to your father, I can do that now on the phone. If he's in physical danger, that's another story. Otherwise, I'll be back in town on Thursday."

"You can't just leave."

"You mean fuck you and leave?"

"We need you now, Lucas."

"Thursday morning. Have him in my office at ten o'clock, nine-thirty, so that he can miss some of the traffic coming in from Jersey."

"How did you know…"

"Jaimie. It's the phone number you're calling from. Meanwhile, if you need me, page me. I'll get right back to you."

"Okay," she said. And she hung up.

Rook went to his desk and took out some index cards. He was going to open a file and charge the guy. Give him a discount because of Jaimie. All he had was the last name and phone number. He jotted some notes on a card he marked "M" and poured himself another beer.

The Man in the Iron Mask was on, and he watched some as he packed. In addition to his business gun, he brought a second .45 and his anklepiece. He packed his sap gloves, plastic handcuffs, and a taser with enough voltage to take down an elephant or Big Earl.

The expectation of getting even got Rook going so that he couldn't sleep. He lay down, but got back up and cleaned his guns. He thought about calling Catherine Wren, but put the receiver down.

The phone rang. It was Jaimie. "I wrote Dad for some Xanax. I wish you were here," she said and she hung up.

Rook went out onto the patio. The lights next door were off. He listened to the traffic and watched the office cleaners in the building across the way. In the distance he could see where the twin towers were gone but somehow still there.

Lucas awoke at 5:30 and got ready to leave. His piss was almost clear. He walked over to the garage with his collar up against the rain.

Rook found Rosen in the back, working on a '92 Cadillac. "You're up early, Sid," he said.

"Got some time to catch up on, Lucas boy."

The dog trotted over to get his head scratched.

"Meant to tell you I appreciate it, Lucas."

"I didn't…"

Rosen put his wrench down. "Colored detective came by. Said the cocksucker that beat me got himself dead. You know what I mean."

"Wasn't me, Sid."

"Of course it wasn't," Rosen said. "Rain's coming up. You want something holds the road."

"Need some cargo space and maybe off road."

Sid underhanded some keys. "Got an SUV, back seat goes down. Plus it got wide tires. Just don't be cornering too quick. You going for breakfast first, bring me back something and couple strips of bacon for my partner here."

"I'll do that, Sid. Going over Oren's and get some coffee."

When he got to Joe's, the place was locked. He walked around the back, but there was no answer. Something wasn't right.

Lucas went to the croissant joint that had opened up around the block. The guy behind the counter tried equally hard to wait on customers and to pretend that he was straight.

A guy in a hard hat ordered an "Allie McBeal" and a "Six Foot Under."

"Can't decide between an Elizabeth Taylor and a Michael Jackson. You do eggs?" Rook said.

"No we don't. Just coffee, tea, and pastries."

"McDonald's it is, friend," Rook said. "Give my regards to Judy Garland."

He went up the street to get some Mc-Something or other and bad coffee. Shirl was stacking up the papers. Her face was bruised and puffy. "Lover's quarrel," she said. Rook nodded and went by.

He dropped the food off at Sid's and drove by the shine stand on his way back out of the city. It was closed because of the rain that had come up. Lucas called Oren's, but got no answer.

Joe called him back in twenty minutes. "It's my Mary Jean," he said. "My Jeanie. I had to take her over to St. Vincent's this morning. She got bad stomach pains, diarrhea and all. I think maybe it's her appendix."

Rook's Bronco hydroplaned on the wet road. "Tell the doc to run a tox screen, Joe. He'll know what this is. Tell him to check for poison."

☙   ☙   ☙

Webster Clark had a chill he cold not shake. Zero to the bone. Virginia roasted the bancha tea for him, and he drank it slowly from the wooden cup. Nothing impure while he fought the poison cancer. Antioxidants, Cat's Claw, macrobiotics, fasting. The chemicals that made him puke his guts out hadn't worked. The microsurgery. The radiation beam. Clinical trials with the doctors' poisons.

He knew he was dying, but he had things to do. And he never let Virginia know.

"How's my girl?" he asked.

"You should sleep, Web. I'll wake you in an hour."

He got off the couch. "Let's go for a walk. I want to see if that groundhog's back."

She tried to smile. "Remember when I ran over that big one with the mower?"

Webster Clark put on his coat. Virginia had a matching one. They looked like two hunters as they went outside.

A chipmunk ran out from the little wall that terraced their garden.

"They're back, Web. That's a good omen. We thought they were all gone."

The branches of the locust tree moved in the wind and made a singing sound.

"You going in tomorrow?" Virginia asked.

"I have some things to do. They're supposed to have some numbers for me." He picked up one of the seed pods from the locust tree and broke it open as they walked up their little hill. "I think maybe I should ratchet things down. Maybe do some consulting work."

"I could go back to teaching."

"You loved Emily Dickinson, but you hated grading papers. Everything's fine, Virginia."

They went back inside. Web went upstairs to pack. She called to him at dinner time, but he had fallen asleep. Virginia put the comforter over her husband and sat with him.

It was 2:00 AM when Webster Clark awoke. He had sweated through his clothes again. His wife was asleep in the brocade chair. Web put Virginia to bed and went downstairs to clean his gun. He knew what had to be done. And it wouldn't be any more difficult than it was to find the feral traitor, Treaster, who had ordered his poison cookbook from the back of a magazine.

CHAPTER 26

The detectives called it "à la mode," when you had a case to clear and something personal on the side. Like when McCullagh got to bring in the dirt-bag who had scammed his sister-in-law. With no help at all, the guy fell down the steps and broke both legs.

The upstate fuckers were going to pay for having gotten Sid Rosen. And if they had anything to do with Jeanie Oren getting sick, they were going to get a fatal dose of what Catherine Wren called his "private justice."

The second scoop of ice cream on this job was getting some rhythm from the Feds. Rook called Warren Phelps to tell him he had something to give a hard on to the showboat FBI agent. Maybe give a chubby to that blimp, Alan Sharkey, that there was some terrorist cult doing crimes across state lines. Phelps' secretary said he was in Palm Beach trying a case. A case of Dom Perignon maybe. Lucas said he'd call back.

He drove straight to the Bottle House. Earl Joost's phone wasn't answering, and he needed to find out more about those scrotes with the brands on their arms. The rain turned to snow as Lucas drove on. He had to stop twice and clear the windshield wipers. There was three inches on the ground when he arrived.

Lucas drove up to the security booth. The same old man ate an egg sandwich. They went through the same shit as before, even though Rook already had his driver's license out.

"Who's Ms. Charney?" the old man said.

"She's the Director of Human Resources."

"You sure of that?"

"As sure as I've been here the last couple days and you like your fried egg sandwiches cold."

"Like 'em hot or cold. Pull over up against the building there. Make sure to stay within them lines."

"I take my job serious," the security guard on the inside said again as he showed Rook where to sign in the book. "You back again?"

"Seems so," Lucas said. He went up the inside iron steps and down the hall. Martha Brookhouser was firmly ensconced in her outer office, even more smug than last time.

"Good morning, Ms. Brookhouser," he said.

"Ms. Charney expecting you?"

"I'll be happy to wait, dear. Perhaps you and I could chat a bit."

"I don't think so," she said.

Edna Charney saw him in twenty minutes. "I'm sorry, I've been in conference. We didn't know whether you were coming back or not. I told Mrs. Politte I had given you everything you needed."

Lucas Rook took out his gold shield. "You did, did you?"

"I'd like to see that identification, Mr. Rook."

"I'm sure you would, Edna. Just like I'm sure you would like to cooperate in this investigation."

He could see the wheels inside her pussy-eating head turning. Who got the bigger cock, or do I just help bust the bad guys? That would give her something to tell some sweet little whore. "What kind of investigation are we talking about, Mr. Rook?"

Rook's cell phone rang.

"This is called classified, Ms. Charney. I'm going to have to step outside."

"You called?" Attorney Warren Phelps said. "You said it was important. You haven't…"

"No, Warren, I haven't shot any old ladies today. Maybe tomorrow."

"You shouldn't jest."

"Not at your rates, I shouldn't, counselor."

Rook filled him in about the whackos with the brands on their arms. Maybe he could get some rhythm from Epps or the big balloon, Alan Sharkey. Phelps inquired whether or not he should talk to Mrs. Politte or her counsel.

"Trolling for new business, Warren?"

"Never at the expense of old clients, Lucas Rook. Let me know what more you turn up. At the least, we want to show the U.S. Attorney our good intentions."

Rook went back into the office. Edna was eager, so he gave it to her slow.

"Earl Joost been out of work? Hunting accident or whatever, Ms. Charney?"

"Yes, he has been."

"Earl Joost was shot in the left foot while avoiding apprehension by federal authorities for his involvement in interstate conspiracy."

She began drumming her big fingers on the desk. "What kind of conspiracy?"

"I'm not at liberty to say anything further at this time, Edna. But we're going to need your help."

"Is it drugs?"

"I can't say at this moment. I need to find Earl Joost, 'Big Earl' they call him. And anybody who you know that associates with him, Jack Curran, or…" He pretended to look at his notes. "A Calvin Treaster. We have reason to believe they may have branded themselves as part of some initiation rite."

Ms. Charney buzzed her receptionist. "Ms. Brookhouser, please tell me where Earl Joost asked we send his checks."

Martha buzzed her back shortly. "He's staying at his mother's on River Road," Ms. Charney said.

"His mother's, how nice," Rook said.

She wrote down the address and handed it over. "We believe in family values here in Oneonta, Mr. Rook."

I bet you do, he thought. As long as you can strap it on. "About those brands, Edna?"

"I've been thinking about that. People talk in a small town. I heard there was a kind of organization up here. For men only, an exclusionary practice which I do not support. Something about the Half Moon, which Calvin Treaster was involved with."

Rook nodded as if it wasn't new to him. "That is correct," he said.

She stood up behind her desk. "Something to do with Henry Hudson, his ship, The Half Moon, and so on. This is a very historical area up here, as you know. It never affected the men's work here at the plant, so I did not take much notice."

Rook made a show of putting his notebook away. "Very good, Edna. Anything else you can think of will be very helpful. In the meantime, you are to keep this conversation completely confidential." He took a step forward. Edna Charney took a step back.

"I understand," she said.

"Under penalty of law," he told her.

She nodded, filled with self-importance and worry.

As Rook left her office, the shop steward walked up.

"Buy you a cup of coffee?" Lucas asked him.

They walked back to the vending machine. Lazy Eye Duffy was

there with his cardboard box. The Steward gave him a hard look and he skittered away.

"You about done here, Mr. Rook?"

"Why's that?"

He sipped his coffee. "Don't like anything bothers my people."

"Like the Half Moon?"

"Including them. I told you when you first started up in here to watch out for them brothers." Wright smiled and shook his head. "That's your police prejudice showing now, isn't it? I say 'brothers' and you thought I'm talking about we people of color." He shook his head. "I was talking about the Brothers of the Half Moon up in here. They haven't tried a way to scare you back to New York City, they will."

"You?"

"Nobody scares me anywhere. And it's been tried. You feel me?"

"I feel you," Rook said. "Maybe I'll see you around, Mr. Wright."

"Maybe not," the Steward said.

Rook went to pay a visit to Earl Joost. Time to roust Big Earl and get at Calvin Treaster. If things went just right, he could continue billing Mrs. Politte while he beat the hell out of them.

River Road was twenty minutes outside of town. Houses on stilts and little pieces of shoreline for weekend vacationers. Big Earl Joost was out on the deck catching a smoke. His foot was in a cast.

Rook came through the front door. Joost's mother napped on the sofa in front of Judge Judy. Big Earl was not happy to see him. "What the fuck?"

Lucas snatched his crutch. "Quiet, Brother Earl. Your mom is sound asleep in there."

Earl Joost tried to get up, but Rook motioned him down with his .45. "Brother Joost. We're going to have a little chat. I'm going to ask you some questions. You clam up on me or lie, I'm absolutely going to blow your other foot off. My little popgun put you in that cast, imagine what this cannon's going to do."

"I'm not telling you nothing."

Lucas cocked the hammer back. "You're going to be a cripple, Earl. No more sunny days at the Bottle House. No more square dancing."

"I don't know nothing."

Rook walked over close. "I might shoot your mom while she's sleeping. I just might do that."

"You wouldn't!"

Lucas turned to go into the living room. "Watch me," he said.

Big Earl turned white. "What do you want to know?"

"Your brand, the Brothers of the Half Moon. All that poison you been spreading around." Rook shoved his big automatic in Earl's face and then his gold badge.

"I'm just muscle. I'm a big guy. I do what he tells me to. Never did anything more than that." He lit another cigarette with Rook watching every move. "All this Henry Hudson, 9-11, I don't even understand it. You go see Calvin Treaster."

"Where's he live, Big Earl?"

"Over on the west side. I never been there, but he works over at the Dye House, also over at Cooperstown sometimes. You go see him." He tried to push himself up. "And leave my mother alone."

"That's up to you and Calvin." Rook smiled. "So if I were you, Earl, I wouldn't tell Calvin Treaster I was coming. I'll let myself out nice and quiet so that I don't disturb Mother. She looks so cozy lying there."

CHAPTER 27

Rook found Calvin Treaster by accessing a detective's favorite research tool, the phone book. There was no one at the single grey house except the three dogs that chased him as he gave the place the once-over. A metal front door. The windows had good locks. A sense of bad around the place, like maybe there was a shotgun hooked up if you tried to get in.

Lucas drove over to the Dye House, a four-story brick building with smoke stacks coming out. There was a new fence all around and a parking lot in the back. On his second passby, he saw Turkey Neck's truck.

No way he wasn't going to send things in the wrong direction if he worked the Dye House like he had the Bottle House. Lucas pulled his Crown Vic to the first bend in the abandoned railroad tracks. If the workers noticed him at all, they'd figure he was either the local police or some guy getting a little car sex, or both.

There was a corrugated overhang left over from the days that trains meant something, and old rain dripped down on the trunk of Rook's car. Like any cop on a stakeout, he took advantage of the distraction to keep from falling asleep. He counted the hits on his car in groups of ten, up until a hundred and then over again. At about eight hundred, a group of men in rubber boots and smocks came marching from the Dye House to Bumpers.

All of them had their heads wrapped in hats of a sort: baseball caps with brims cut off, orange hunting hats with the earflaps up and down, two filthy derbies, and on one tall man, a top hat. A John Deere hat came by, but it was worn by a young blonde man with a handlebar moustache.

Rook watched the door in case Turkey Neck came out, but when the group made their rowdy exodus from the converted railroad shed, Calvin Treaster was not with them.

Plan B meant drinking a cold beer in a pig sty. The same bartender poured and called out the time. Shop Steward Wright was there, exercising the special privileges to make sure all the stragglers got back to work.

"Well, shamus," he said. "What brings you back to this fine emporium?"

"Don't look Irish to me," said Georgie White. "And I should know. My brother-in-laws, they're all micks."

Wright shook his head. "The other kind of shamus. Like from noir films. Isn't that right, Mr. Rook?"

"Draft and a bump," Lucas said.

Jack Moore walked in. His face reddened. "You here again? I thought I…"

"Just here for a cold draft and a VO before I head on back."

"Don't let the swinging door hit you in the ass on the way out," Jack Moore said.

"Any trouble, Jack?" Georgie asked. "You only get surly when you've had six or so."

"Pour me my drink, Georgie boy. I ain't causing no commotion and I don't give a damn."

"Last round, people," the steward called. "Otherwise you're us-ing leave time. I'm heading back. You're not with me when I cross the tracks, you're on your own."

Lazy Eye and somebody he hadn't seen before made it to their feet.

"You walking out, Lucas Rook?" Wright said. "Or you making this your home?"

"One and done, Mr. Wright," Lucas said. "Jack Moore, you take it easy. Sorry for your troubles."

Rook went back to his car and placed a call to the Hall of Fame in Cooperstown. "Calvin Treaster?" he asked the office.

"We don't allow personal calls."

"It's not exactly personal. My wife and son were in the other day. Stevie knocked over a whole display. You people were very nice about it. They both had Dodgers hats on, Martha and little Stevie, the retro kind. I was born in Brooklyn actually. Anyway, we went up the street to eat and when we came back, someone was pulling out of the lot, and I guess I wasn't paying attention, talking about Sandy Koufax and Don Drysdale and all and I hit him, I'm sorry to say, and I said I'd pay what it cost or turn it into my insurance company which… Anyway, I never got to apologize for the mess my boy made, which he had to clean up, Mr. Treaster, I mean."

"He's working night work, sir, and now if you'll excuse me."

Rook mumbled something and hung up. He had a couple of stops to make. He called over to the funeral home, but the owner was making a house call, so he drove back down the road to the County Health. The hourly rate and the mileage were good. He called into Attorney Eck on the way to Oneonta.

"Kipps, Wetherill, and Hobbes."

"Arthur Eck, please."

He was transferred to the attorney's secretary. "Who shall I say is calling?"

"Lucas Rook."

"May I ask what matter you are calling in reference to?"

"Mr. Eck will know."

"I'm sorry, Mr. Eck is not in."

"Just tell him I called." Terrific business, everybody will be charging Mrs. Politte for something that didn't happen.

The Mohawk was behind the counter at the County office. An old woman in a tight sweater came up. "May I help you?" she asked.

"I'm working on it already, Betty," the Mohawk said. "We're up and running," he told Rook. "What can I get you?"

"Need a run on facilities, subsets acute gastric illness or poisoning in the last ninety days."

"Quick as you can say 'Diablo Two.'"

Rook looked at him.

"Computer game," he said over his shoulder. He came back in a matter of moments. "We had seven fatalities meet the criteria of gastric illness. Nothing for poisonings."

"Can you break it down any further?" Rook asked.

"We have five male, two female, one was a minor child."

"How about by occupations?" Lucas asked.

"Adults obviously. All I can give you is what was inputted from the death certificates or whatever." He went back to his screen. "We got factory worker or dye worker. One of them said 'machine operator.'"

"Thanks," Rook said.

"Don't mention it," the Mohawk said. "Here's a printout. And thanks for not saying 'How, Chief,' and all that."

Lucas took the paperwork. He'd write up the interview and start a digest of the material he just received. Then start on his interim bill, have a nice steak somewhere and meet with Turkey Neck. Proper investigative technique required that he completely rule out foul play by asking Turkey Neck some hard questions. Rook had no reason to believe the inquiry would go anywhere, but it would give him the opportunity of beating the hell out of Calvin Treaster.

Hawkeye's was as good a place as anywhere else. The green-eyed hostess was glad to see him. "Well, how are you?" she said.

Lucas smiled at the cleavage she was arching in his direction.

"Well how are you, Terry?"

"I'm sure glad to be seeing you again. It's kind of like we're old friends, you know what I mean?" she said.

Rook looked over at Pat, who was gesturing him to a table.

Patel had his thick black hair in a mullet. "You like my new look?" he asked. "Business in the front. Party in the back."

"You were any more American, Pat, you'd be wearing a ten-gallon hat."

The waiter went away for a moment and returned with bread, water, the menu, and a cold beer. "I don't understand 'ten gallon hat,'" he said.

"It doesn't matter, Pat. Chill out."

Patel came closer to the table. "'Chill out.' In Sanskrit, the ancient language, we say 'shantih, shantih' – 'The peace that passeth all understanding.'"

"My brother once busted a bad guy named Shantih."

"Peace and blessings on you and your brother, sir."

"Not really," Rook said and he drank the beer.

CHAPTER 28

Calvin Treaster knew that the Jews in Washington were going to take his social security and use it to make their payments to their hooked-nose brothers. Anything that was left, they'd give to their boney-ass wives and homo boyfriends in Hollyweird.

He had known that since he heard about the banks going bust in the thirties. The stock market crash was just a way to get the prices way low so they could buy everything up dirt cheap. You relied on the government and social security, you were going to wind up as poor as Henry Fonda and the rest of the Jobs in *Grapes of Wrath*. The government and the foreigners would see to that. You'd wind up set adrift to die, like Henry Hudson in the Half-Moon.

Calvin Treaster knew this from when he was first old enough to make cash money. He didn't trust banks because the only interest bankers had was an interest in what you were doing and how they were going to spend what you were making. At first and for a long time he buried his money in coffee cans. "Good to the Last Drop."

He smiled with his crooked teeth.

Even after his wife left, Calvin worked two jobs while his daughter went up the road, at first to his sister-in-law's and then to Mrs. Leonard's, who raised her big family and Peanut as if she were her own. He worked at the dye house since he was twenty-three, and for a long time at the filling station and at the Howard Johnson's Restaurant on the Interstate before he got the job at Cooperstown. With his extra money, he bought things he could touch. Gold coins, hand-tooled firearms, and his house that was on a narrow strip of land near the road.

The part-time job at the Hall of Fame was a good one because he could get the hours doing maintenance, setting up displays, and sometimes nightwatchman work, which usually came on days after the holidays and on the weekends. The set-up for the two new play-ers voted in to the Hall was running behind since they messed things up in the office. This meant he got to put in two straight days of double shifts, which he worked by taking some leave from the Dye House.

Gary Carter was a big mouth, but he was smart. You could tell by how he got himself in playing in Canada and then Jew York, and then just to make sure he had everything covered, he played in both the Hollywood fag towns. Eddie Murray was just another sullen nigger, who didn't appreciate that if they weren't bred strong as slaves, they wouldn't be nothing at all. Steve Garvey, Dale Murphy, they were players should have gotten in. Thank God at least all them Latin players didn't get the votes.

Lucas Rook drove around the Hall of Fame so he could see the employees' parking lot. There was the truck with the liberty tree decal on the back. He parked a block away and came through the black iron gates, hoping to get Calvin Treaster as he was coming out.

Rook bought a New York Giants reprint yearbook across the

street. Willie Mays, Monte Irvin, a picture of Sal "The Barber" Maglie, who could shave the edges of the plate like a master, but who always needed a shave himself. The Shot Heard Round the World and Dusty Rhoads, who thrilled the world and then drove a bus at the World's Fair.

Closing time had come and gone, but not Turkey Neck. Rook went inside. "We're closed, sir," said a man with a droopy eye.

"Left my new Angels hat," Lucas said as he rushed by. He went into the men's room and waited until they came to shut off the lights.

He heard voices. Two men working and a woman leaving. Lucas came out and moved through the displays, past the silver bats and the webless gloves. Joe D's streak, flannel uniforms, baseballs from all the no-hitters. Congressman Bunning's perfect game on Father's Day.

He positioned himself in the alcove for the Negro Leagues and leaned against the memorial to Cool Papa Bell. Thirty minutes went by, enough time for Turkey Neck and whoever to get used to their routine. Rook followed the voices. One was coming from where the pictures of postage stamps were hung. Calvin's voice came from downstairs.

Rook went after him. The basement was well lit. The air conditioner hummed. Except for the care with which the equipment was stored, it might have been a sporting goods store.

Treaster napped against a shelf of baseball shoes, his John Deere hat down over his eye. Rook came on him with his .45. He put the muzzle to Turkey Neck's head. "Rise and shine," he said.

Calvin's answer was to spit.

"That's a fifty-dollar fine on top of everything else. Going to be an expensive night."

He spit again.

"You're an evil man," Lucas said as he cocked the hammer. "Sneaking around to poison folks."

Treaster tilted his hat back and gave Rook a smile with his crooked teeth.

"You're all by yourself, Calvin boy, just you and me. Nobody here to back you up."

"What you going to do? It's way too late for you and yours." Treaster rolled up his sleeve to show his tattoo.

"I'm going to blow your head off," Rook said.

"No you ain't. You're going to arrest me or something. Maybe rough me up a bit."

Lucas brought the barrel across Calvin's head. Treaster slumped, but just as quick came up strong with a knife from inside his boot.

Rook blocked it with his arm, but lost his gun. Calvin Treaster jumped up quick. "Got a head as thick as a cannon ball." Treaster grabbed a heavy bat from off the rack. "Not going to get in close where you can use your billy club. You going to stop me, you're going to use the ankle gun you shot Big Earl with. Most likely you be the one to go to jail." He swung the bat hard and low.

Lucas went back against the shelf of baseball shoes. Treaster attacked from left to right and back again as he moved in. "I seen you with your cane," he said. "Going to cripple you up for good."

Rook stepped inside and slashed down. The metal spikes tore at Calvin's face.

"I am a Brother of the Half Moon!" screamed Turkey Neck. "A brother you left to die."

Rook brought the shoe down again and again. Again and again.

CHAPTER 29

Lucas Rook had worked a thousand crime scenes, so it took him only moments to turn the scene into a robbery. All around him were portable items of great value. Since there was no way of telling whether the display cases were alarmed, Lucas took the spikes he had beaten Calvin Treaster with, and two other pairs of shoes from the '50s. There was a bin of baseballs to his left, and he took an Eddie Mathews bat.

Rook went up the stairs quick, listening for the other worker. Maybe the doors were alarmed or the memorabilia would set off his sensors. A gray-haired man had the back door open so he could catch a smoke. Rook waited until he was done and then went back outside through the closing door to the small park in the rear.

A half dozen grungy teens were drinking beer and smoking reefer up against the Fenimore Cooper statue. A girl with purple hair rode the statue's foot like it was a bucking horse.

"Do it, Violet, do it!" one yelled.

"Ride me, ride me, girl," yelled another.

Rook shined his maglite on them. "Okay, kiddies, the party's over."

"I don't think so," said the one with the Army coat.

"Oh, boy," said another. "Rent-a-cop going to call my mommy?"

Lucas tilted his light so they could see his .45. "Nope," he said. "My squad's going to run you up to Albany. Violet, girl, you're going to ride with me. My lieutenant's going to do the driving."

"You ain't no staties," the one without the shirt dared.

"You're right," Rook said. "You're desecrating an official landmark. Uncle Sam considers that terrorism." He started running in, waving his light back and throwing the Marichal ball into the bushes to the left and the Robin Roberts to the right.

The punks scattered. They would be a logical choice for the museum crime. Rook left the Mathews bat around the corner and the bloody shoe down the block as he drove out of town.

❧   ❧   ❧

When he got back to his room at the Clarion, Rook called Joe Oren. "She's still in intensive care, Lucas. My little girl. She's so pale."

"Did you…"

"I asked them about the poison thing, Lucas. They said they knew what they were doing. I actually had to grab some jerkwad by the neck for him to order a test for it. They said it came back negative. What's all this about?"

"The usual paranoia, Joe." Rook turned on the television. "Jeanie'll be okay. I got another couple of days here. I'll be back."

"She better be," Joe said. "I'm a bag of nothing, she's not."

"She got to be," Lucas said. "We're getting married. Remember?"

"God forbid, Rook," Oren tried to laugh. "God forbid."

Rook showered thoroughly and washed his hair. He cleaned his nails, wiped off his shoes and drove over to Hawkeye's for something to eat.

No Terry with the great legs and great eyes. The hostess was a black-haired girl with too much make-up. He looked over. Patel wasn't there either. The waiter looked like Nick Nolte. "My name's Maggie," the hostess said. "Some people call me Magdalena though."

She smiled and turned her head a little bit. Rook followed her gaze. Terry was sitting at the bar in low-rise pants and a see-through blouse. "She said she hoped you was coming in tonight. It's her night off."

"That's a good thing, Magdalena. A night off's a good thing."

Rook went over to the bar. Terry held her cigarette for him to light. "I'm having white wine like in New York. Are you glad to see me?"

"I'm glad to see you, Terry. I am. You want to grab dinner?"

"I'm not supposed to be here. You know, with the customers." She sipped her drink. "You still read minds?"

"You want to get out of here."

Terry took a last drag on her Marlboro Light and snubbed it out. "I know a nice place nearby," she said. "You drive." She walked ahead of him to show all she had. "It's real nice. Back up the road to the left," she said.

When they got in his car, she put her hand on his leg.

Lucas pretended to swerve the wheel. "Going to have a car accident, Astoria, Queens."

"Aren't you sweet?" she said. She pointed to a closed car dealership on the right. "We can't have that now, can we?"

By the time Rook pulled in and away from the lights, she had it out. "My, my," she said. "There's a lot of you." She brushed her hair away from her face and started with her tongue. Twirling strokes first. Then long slow licks before she took him in her mouth. She used her hand to pump him, then shut it off so that when he came she got all of it. Terry made little moaning sounds when she swallowed.

She took a mint from her purse. "Was that good for you?" she asked.

"You made my day," he said.

"Good," she said. "I'm glad."

The restaurant she took them to tried the bullfight theme, steaks and so on. "How about surf and turf?" Rook asked her. Mrs. Politte was paying. "As I remember, it's a favorite in Astoria, Queens. And another glass of white wine."

Terry unzipped his pants again in the parking lot.

"These seats go back," Rook told her.

"Not on the first date," she said. "Just drive." When they got back to Hawkeye's, she had him park in the back next to her car.

She unlaced her top. "Would you like to see my tits?" Terry licked her fingers and touched her nipples. They stood erect and firm. She leaned over and slid the seat back. "They're real," she said. "Fuck my tits. Fuck my tits."

Lucas reached for her crotch. "Not the first date," she said again. And she used her hands and breasts to get him off, doing her own nipples as she did, making herself come in rapid gasps.

Terry turned on the inside light. She gathered up all the jism from off her ample breasts and licked it down. "Did you foresee that, Mr. Fortune Teller?" she asked.

"I saw me fucking you for sure."

She opened his car door. "I get off tomorrow at ten. I'll lay you till you scream."

Rook would have liked to tap that good, but his plans were a follow-up at the Bottle House and then an interview with the sex harasser, Carillo. He knew that both were bullshit, but a good final report could mean more work later. He went back to the Clarion and showered. Then he went to sleep.

Lucas had breakfast in the coffee shop. Ham and eggs and a side of grits. The waitress appeared to be the owner's wife. His name was Kumar and he brought Rook a free bowl of fresh fruit compliments of the house.

At the next table were sales reps from an engineering firm. They ate from the buffet line and argued about the Giants and the Jets. A man chased his kids to the outside pool.

Lucas checked his messages. Attorney Eck called to confirm he received the first draft of the preliminary report and that he would be approving additional retainer funds. The funeral director had nothing to add to the investigation other than that he had a sale on pre-paid cremations and the deluxe coffin package included a "This is your Life" video.

Everything that Rook had turned up led to the conclusion that the deaths at Mrs. Politte's factory were not intentional. The data from the Public Health Department did not indicate criminal activity or that the gastric illness fatalities were particular to the Bottle House. And his interviews of two physicians, the HR Department, the shop steward and numerous employees did not indicate foul play at the factory.

Calvin Treaster and his redneck boys were characters right out of the movie *Deliverance*. That two of them who came after him worked at the Bottle House was the kind of thing you could expect in a factory town. It was cult shit and territorial violence he was looking at. No way was that part of the case he was working.

🌾 🌾 🌾

The egg sandwich man was not at the front gate when Lucas arrived at the Bottle House. His replacement waved Rook through without looking up. The inside guard sucked on a piece of straw and read a magazine. Rook signed in and went up the fire stairs.

Martha Brookhouser sat smugly at her desk. "Ms. Charney is

not in, Mr. Rook, so I'm not sure that I can help you."

"Security man at the gate and downstairs weren't downstairs either. Anything wrong here, Martha?"

Her jaw set. "I told you…"

Rook went over and sat in the chair next to her desk. "Right, right. Is there a funeral or something, Ms. Brookhouser?"

She moved some papers back and forth on her desk. "It's the opening of deer season, Mr. Rook."

"I see, I see. Well, just dial Ms. Charney on her cellular. Another hour and a half at the most, I'm out of here for good."

"I don't…"

"Do yourself a favor, Marty, call her up and get my wise-cracking New York self out of here."

Martha Brookhouser went into the HR Director's office and placed a call. She came back out and got Rook the pile of files he had seen before. He took them next door, put his feet up and dozed until it was time to go.

Rook brought the material back to Ms. Brookhouser in an hour. "It was a pleasure meeting you, Martha. I'm only sorry I missed seeing Edna in her hunting outfit. She must be a heart stopper."

Since he was still on the clock, Lucas stopped by the Clarion and then took the long way back by the Garden State Parkway. He'd close out the job tomorrow. Then draft a closing report for the lawyer's review and his final bill. When he got paid, he'd send Scanagi a special pizza from Checchia's.

Lucas had lunch with Sid Rosen and went over to 166 to check his mail. He bought himself that pair of shoes and then took his brother's Avanti for a run.

❦   ❦   ❦

Webster Clark awoke in the night. His wife turned toward him in her sleep, and he remained for a while so that they could stay together like the pieces of a puzzle. Then while Virginia slept, he changed into his office clothes, a gray suit, a nice white shirt, and, as always, a bow tie. He picked the one with the purple dots she bought for him last week.

The heat in the kitchen had not kicked on yet, and as Web went down the back stairs, he felt the cold come up to meet him. He put a muffler around his neck and stood by the stove as he made himself a cup of tea. Then he took his morning pills and left for work, stopping for a moment at the door to listen to Virginia's calm and rhythmic breaths.

The sun was just coming up as he started on the same route he always took. Down Greenhill Road to Crescent and on to the Southway. It was early so that the traffic on 295 and US 50 flowed smoothly. Two trucks passed by, the back one carrying fine meats. It was the same model and color as the one he had intercepted on the way to New York City from Oneonta with its load of poison diet bars.

Hadley was at the duty desk when Webster Clark arrived at the Institute. "A long day, Web?" he asked.

"A long day, Skip." Clark went up into his office. Somehow in the early light, it still looked the same. The photos on the wall, the flag, the pictures on his desk of him and Virginia in fishing hats and the one of their dog that died. The Wilton rug he brought from home.

He had papers to go over and a memo to draft. Then the pain was on him fast, like a broken glass. The shadow of the agony that used to warn him first was no longer there.

Webster Clark knew that the cancer and the treatments had killed part of him and that the Percocet no longer worked. He took a Dilaudid and waited for the narcotizing wave of warmth. When the pain had dulled, he finished the memo and went back out.

"Have a nice day," Hadley said as Clark checked out.

"You too, Skip. You too."

Web left his Saturn wagon in the garage and took one of the Institute's black Mercury sedans. He waved to the closed circuit as he pulled away.

He had an operation to finish. Like sitting in the jungle rain, wrapping himself in the jungle night. Sliding, hiding in the jungle night. Blood shining in the dark. Living apart and watching the Agent Orange rain come down like soda pop.

Like the Dugway Proving Grounds. The sky shut down. The Great Salt Lake Desert all around, the foxes on Five Mile Hill hiding from the poison gas. Where all the air was scrubbed and burned. Poison for sale like gallons of paint for the armies of the night, the armies of the light.

Like tracing Thomas Lavy down and hanging him in his cell without a word before he strung him up. And killing killers before they could poison reservoirs.

He had this last thing to do, clean up the ricin poison and the poisoners. He was all but done.

CHAPTER 30

Rook was glad to be back in the City. He had the appointment with Jaimie's father. Afterwards, he'd run out to get that last statement from Frank Carillo. With some luck he'd bring in some more new business. At the least, Grace had been talking about driving her on some of her photography sessions, and with the money she was getting per shoot, it could be worth it as fill-in.

Jimbo Turner brushed a customer's hat as Rook came up. "Why thank you, sir," he said with a little flourish of his hand and a salute with his whisk broom. Rook got up on the stand and handed over the box of new shoes.

"First shine on these, Mr. Rook?"

"Yes, sir, Jimbo Turner. What's happening on your street?"

"As quiet as a man jerking off while his wife's in bed." He ran his fingers over Rook's shoes. "You been rough on these. Don't be washing them down so hard. Bring 'em in, let me clean 'em up." He took a can from behind the stand and tipped it onto his cleaning rag.

"Using naphtha here, so don't be lighting up, no smoke or letting anybody do it close up. We all go in flames like my friend Mazmanian. He was a floor man. Worked the old way. Always stripped them down with naphtha. New helper comes by and lights his smoke, no more Mazmanian."

Jimbo wiped the shoes clean and rubbed the first coat of polish in with his long fingers. Then he worked the rag and brushes, snapping and clacking as he finished. The shineman changed the laces and handed up the old ones.

Lucas used his cane to help himself down. The shineman used his whisk on Rook's windbreaker. "Man could use some Jersey tomatoes and sweet corn when the spring comes round," he said.

Rook went over to Oren's. The Spanish counter girl was there with Sam. He came out when he saw Lucas. "They's still at St. Vincent's. Mr. Joe been there all night," Sam said. "You going over, take him something from here. Hospital food's so bad it makes you sick."

Lucas had two fried eggs with the yolks broken. The coffee was good. He took the brown bag from Sam and went over to the hospital.

He found Joe in the pastel lounge down the hall and handed him the paper bag. Joe took the coffee, but left the food.

"She's still in ICU, Lucas. It's looking better, but they don't know what it is." He sat down. "The bleeding's stopped."

"You need anything done, Joe?"

The big freckled man got up and went down the hall. "She's my little girl," he said.

Rook arrived at his office in time to straighten up for his appointment with Mesoros. Mail stuffed in the slot. Another monthly payment on a two-year-old invoice. A check for thirty dollars to change phone service for the tenth time.

The bathroom needed paper towels. The loony photographer

next door was yelling "Croatan!" over and over as Lucas left for the store.

Lucas got back with ten minutes to spare. He waited for Jaimie's father, but no one showed. After forty-five minutes, he went over to Rosen's to get his car.

Sid had a white Lincoln up on the lift and was draining out the oil. "Looks like the Great White Whale, doesn't it?" he said.

"You Captain Ahab, Sid?"

"Not me. You going out?"

Rook sat down at Rosen's desk and propped up his leg. "Running out to take a statement. If you want, I'll drop you at the mall and get you on the way back."

"I'm good, Lucas, boy."

"Good, Sid," Rook said. He left for Lawrenceville, New Jersey to take Frank Carillo's statement.

Lucas thought about Catherine as he drove on to the sex harasser's. Her morning run, the gazebo in the back, the smell of lilacs from outside her bedroom window. One time Catherine Wren took Lucas to the fancy school in Lawrenceville to hear Walter Becker lecture. The place was very highbrow, but two knuckleheads tried to swipe a Lexus from the parking lot. It was Becker's with all his papers in the trunk. For once, Catherine Wren appreciated Rook's intolerance for creeps and crime. His exact words which brought the surrender of the vehicle were, "If you two scumbags get out of the car right now, I'll only shoot one of you in the nuts."

MapQuest's directions to Carillo's were on the mark, but traffic was backed up because of the sunglare. When Rook arrived, he cruised around the block twice and parked across the street. He looked at his notes and jotted down "Prepared for interview," for billing purposes. The house was a two-story with vinyl siding. The shades on all the windows were down.

CHAPTER 31

Not many things surprised Lucas Rook any more, and having Jaimie Mesoros answer Frank Carillo's door wasn't going to be one of them.

"Aren't you going to ask me in?" Lucas said.

She hesitated, but when Rook took a step forward, she stood aside. The little house was warm, but there was the smell of disinfectant. A room was off to the left of the narrow hall. A small sofa with a pillow from someone's bed. A recliner with a blanket folded on it.

Lucas leaned on his cane in the narrow hallway. She didn't move.

"Moonlighting with home care, Dr. Mesoros?" he said.

A voice called from upstairs. "Who is it? Who is it?"

"It's okay," she answered. "It's nobody at all. They were just leaving."

"No, no," the voice yelled. A door slammed. Furniture being pushed across the floor.

"See what you've done!" Jaimie said as she ran upstairs.

Rook took the opportunity to go into the kitchen. One of the window shades was taped closed. The other two had remnants of tape on them. He went through the kitchen drawers. Cheap flat-ware with green plastic handles. Another drawer held the usual junk, odds and ends, plastic combs, twine, ball point pens. A third drawer was filled with rolls of tape.

Rook was studying the notes and magnets on the refrigerator when Dr. Mesoros returned. She pointed to his cane leaning against the table. "For dramatic effect, or do you mean to beat my father with it?"

"Calm down," Rook told her. "That's not going to work with me."

Jaimie sat down. She picked at a piece of formica on the chipped table top, then stopped herself. "I used to pick at my nail polish all the time. It made my mother crazy."

"Should I be asking what you're doing here, Jaimie?"

She got up and turned on the gas range. "What are you doing here, Lucas Rook?"

"You asked me to help."

"And now I'm asking you to leave." Jaimie stirred the pot of broth. "You can let yourself out. I expect that you'll be gone when I come back down."

"After you tell me what's going on," Rook said.

"I asked you to leave."

"You asked me to help, Jaimie. You're a no-show for your ten o'clock, and you've been holding out on me who your father is."

"I asked you to help with the problems you are causing."

"I don't like this even a little bit, Jaimie. If you want to tell me what you're talking about, I'll listen, other than that I'm out of here. I don't have time for your being pissed off we got it on a couple times."

"Don't flatter yourself. I fucked you as much as you fucked me."

She turned her back to set a tray and then turned back again. "I'm not stupid. Men like you think women are stupid. You've been following my father, hounding him, spying on him. That's why we didn't come to see you."

Lucas leaned back. "And I would be doing that for what reason?"

"So he would have to hire you." Jaimie Mesoros made fists with her small hands. "Fucking me was a bonus," she said.

"Two strikes, Dr. Mesoros. You want to take another swing? Three strikes and I'm out. You tell me about your father, maybe I can unscramble this. If not, I'm done here. I'm not in the drama business."

Jaimie patted her pocket for the bottle of pills and took the tray upstairs. Rook used the time to check the kitchen cabinets, which were filled with canned soup and more rolls of tape.

When Jaimie returned, she turned on the tea kettle and sat back down. "My father was, is a chemist. He met my mother at work. She died three years ago. I was just finishing med school. He took a teaching job for a year, but he only has a Master's Degree, so he had to take the job at that dirty little factory in Oneonta so we could…" she turned away, "…be a family while I did my residency at the hospital."

"And then what happened?"

"Some dirty little slut at the dirty little factory accused my father of coming on to her. It was ridiculous. Papa was ashamed for the memory of my mother. The Human Resources person hates men, she railroaded it through. He wouldn't even…" She began picking at the formica again.

Rook waited for her to continue.

"They were married for almost thirty years, Lucas. They met at work. She was his secretary at BI."

"Which is?"

"Bach Industries. Dad is a chemist. He did quality control. "She looked away. "I don't understand any of this. I don't understand why you're here."

"I do insurance work, Jaimie. Sometimes I do what they call 'risk management assessments.' I was sent here to interview your father because of the sexual harassment they said happened. As far as I'm concerned, I just did."

"So if you're not following him, Lucas, who is?"

"My guess is nobody is. His nerves, probably. Losing his wife, his job, you're all grown." Rook got up to leave. "But I'll look into it."

"And us?" she asked.

"It was nice, Jaimie. It really was."

Rook went over it as he drove back into the City. Maybe some shyster PI like Womack was salting the mine, putting pressure on Carillo so it looked like he needed to write a big check. More likely Frank Carillo was just nuts. The only thing sticking out of the pile of crap was that Carillo was a chemist. Maybe somehow, some way Jaimie's father had something to do with the deaths at the Bottle House. Loose ends could come around and strangle you. He'd do some research on Bach Industries at Mrs. Politte's generous rates.

Sid was back at the garage eating a plate of smoked fish and potato salad. "You eat?" he asked.

"I'm good," Rook said. "I eat them onions, new business shows up, I asphyxiate them."

"Vic running smooth?"

"Running smooth, Sid."

"You finish that book I gave you?"

"Been on the road. I'll have it back to you next week. Just checking on you, partner. You alright?"

"I'm good." Rosen picked up a piece of the salty fish and a circle of onion. "Cream soda's one of civilization's great accomplishments," he said as he popped open the can.

Lucas walked around to Oren's. He looked like the world had been lifted from his shoulders.

"How's my girl?" Lucas asked.

"Good, good. They figured it out. They told me it was 'SEB' that Jeanie had, some kind of staph infection."

"She coming home soon?"

"Couple of days yet. But you could go over later. She'll be in a regular room."

Rook picked up the menu, then put it down. "Going to run by the office, then I'll check on her, Joe."

"Good," Joe Oren said.

"Good," said Rook.

Rook's beeper started going off as soon as he entered the lobby at 166 Fifth Avenue. It was Jaimie Mesoros, over and over. When he got upstairs, there were four messages from her. His phone rang.

"Please help," she said. "Please. He was here. He is here. I can tell."

"Who, Jaimie? Who's there?"

"The man who's been following my father. He said he's going to kill us."

"Hang up and dial 911. Then lock yourself in the bathroom. Do it!"

Rook raced to the scene like he was answering a call, but knowing somebody might be wanting him in the middle. The nutsy father upstairs, one of the boys left over from Oneonta, maybe somebody with a crazy hard-on about Jaimie. He made a quick pass around the front and back of the house before parking two doors away and coming across the lawn.

The shades were still drawn. There were lights on upstairs and in the kitchen. He could hear someone coming down the steps. The front door was locked. Lucas went around to the back with his hand on his automatic.

An older man opened the door. "Come in, Mr. Rook. I'm glad you're here." Lucas followed him into the warm kitchen. The tea kettle as whistling. Jaimie sat at the little table.

"I understand you two have already met, Mr. Rook. Why don't you sit down. You two have a lot to talk about." He put the sugar bowl and matching cups and saucers on a tray.

"Is everything okay, Jaimie?" Lucas asked.

She didn't answer. Rook watched her hands, waiting for her to pick at the formica.

"Jaimie, you said…."

She sat motionless. Her hands did not move. Rook pushed his chair back a bit.

"Isn't this cozy?" the man with the bowtie said.

"And you're Frank Carillo?" Rook asked.

"Tea's ready. Milk or lemon, Mr. Rook?"

"What's going on here?" Rook said.

"We'll have time to chat before the police get here. Jaimie did not have the opportunity to complete her call, but I've seen to it. My name is Webster Clark." He set the tray down. "You can keep that .45 if it makes you feel comfortable."

"I got A.D.D. when it comes to assholes, Mr. Clark." He spoke to Jaimie without turning. "Your father?"

"He's …" she started.

"I took care of him the way I took care of your friend, Sid Rosen. Only I'm afraid Frank's life is over."

Rook framed a shot at him.

"That brand I placed on the scum who was supposed to have beaten your friend, that was a nice touch, don't you think? It kept you after those cretins in Oneonta."

"You're running out of time," Rook said.

"I've had plenty of time, Lucas Rook, to watch your neighbor, Grace, beautiful, but blind. Your friends, the Orens. And you. The picture of your brother and you on your mantle piece is quite touching."

"Your time is up," Rook said.

"You're right, Lucas Rook. My time is up. The cancer that started in my bladder spread like a bad rumor. My endurance isn't what it used to be so I do appreciate your help, unwitting though it was. We in the espionage business refer to you as an 'asset.'"

Rook adjusted his angle to keep sharp. "Keep talking, scumbag," he said. "So I know how deep to bury you."

"Certainly, Detective. Those half-wits in Oneonta, we people at the Pendle Institute, we're spies you know, we call them 'pig waste.' If all their wild schemes had come to fruition, the Brothers of the Half Moon wouldn't have killed enough people to fill a bus to Staten Island. But they would have scared a hundred million people to death."

"So what's your game, Webster Clark?"

"It's a poison game, Mr. Rook. Those deaths at Mrs. Politte's factory were caused by ricin, a poison made from castor beans. It's easily extracted in a kitchen such as this. Anybody that's been working in the dye industry knows that. Like your friend, the late Calvin Treaster. *Palma Christi*, it's called. The 'Hands of Christ.'" Clark smiled when he said that.

"And what's going on here?"

"She is an innocent, Lucas Rook. And you are a witness."

Rook's hand was at his .45. "To what?"

Webster Clark poured the tea with his right hand and with his left produced a Glock .40.

"To my revenge," he said as he shot Jaimie Mesoros and himself.

Clark slid down against the stove. His pool of blood spread out.

"There will be no secrets, Lucas Rook." He held up his blood red hands. "This is my poison. And my vengeance."

The sirens screamed outside as the squad cars came roaring in, their red lights flashing in the night. The cops could have passed for twins the way they walked and talked. Rook showed them both of his ID's and saved most of what he knew to trade the Feds. No way this wouldn't make his problem with the U.S. Attorney go away.

It started to rain again as Lucas Rook drove back into the City. He thought of Jaimie Mesoros and her father. And Webster Clark, who killed them for his vengeance. He thought about Calvin Treaster, who was an evil man and paid the price.

Rook stopped by the place where his brother, Kirk, had died and headed home.

ADDENDUM

On June 10, 2003, the United States Supreme Court in *Dow Chemical Company v. Stephenson* allowed cancer-stricken Vietnam veterans to proceed for damages caused by Agent Orange decades ago. The deciding action was the recusal of Justice John Paul Stevens, whose only son, a Vietnam veteran, died of cancer in 1996.

MORE LUCAS ROOK

Mark your calendar for the most thrilling Lucas Rook mystery of all!

The world is saddened and terrified when Teacher Janice, the beloved hostess of a long-running children's show, is found beheaded. But the Philadelphia police know something so bizarre and shocking that Inspector Zinn can share it only with Private Detective Lucas Rook.

Publisher's Weekly called Richard Sand's award-winning *Private Justice* "bizarre and, it must be said, rather warped." His next Lucas Rook Mystery makes that seem like a bedtime story: *The Watchman with a Hundred Eyes*, available Summer 2004.

Check out these other fine titles by Durban House
online or at your local book store.

EXCEPTIONAL BOOKS
BY
EXCEPTIONAL WRITERS

NONFICTION

BEHIND THE MOUNTAIN	Nick Williams
FISH HEADS, RICE, RICE WINE & WAR: A VIETNAM PARADOX	Lt. Col. Thomas G. Smith, Ret.
JIMMY CARTER AND THE RISE OF MILITANT ISLAM	Philip Pilevsky
MIDDLE ESSENCE— WOMEN OF WONDER YEARS	Landy Reed
SPORES, PLAGUES, AND HISTORY: THE STORY OF ANTHRAX	Chris Holmes
WHITE WITCH DOCTOR	Dr. John A. Hunt
PROTOCOL Innis,	Mary Jane McCaffree, Pauline

and Richard Sand.

For 25 years, the bible for public relations firms, corporations, embassies, foreign governments, and individuals seeking to do business with the Federal Government.

DURBAN HOUSE FICTION

A DREAM ACROSS TIME   Annie Rogers

Jamie Elliott arrives from New York onto the lush Caribbean island of St. Lucia, and finds herself caught up in Island forces, powerful across the centuries, which find deep echoes in her recurring dreams.

AFTER LIFE LIFE   Don Goldman

A hilarious murder mystery taking place in the afterlife. Andrew Law, Chief Justice of the Texas Supreme Court, is the Picture of robust health when he suddenly dies. Upon arriving in The afterlife, Andy discovers he was murdered, and his untimely has some unexpected, and far-reaching consequences—a worldwide depression, among others. Many diabolical plots are woven in this funny, fast-paced whodunit, with a surprising double-cross ending.

an-eye-for-an-eye.com   Dennis Powell

Jed Warren, Vietnam Peacenik, and Jeff Porter, ex-Airborne, were close friends and executives at Megafirst Bank. So when CEO McAlister crashes the company, creams off millions in bonuses, and wipes out Jed and Jeff, things began to happen.

If you wonder about corporate greed recorded in today's newspapers, read what one man did about it in this intricate, devious, and surprise-ending thriller.

BASHA   John Hamilton Lewis

LA reviewer, Jeff Krieder's pick as "Easily my best read of the year." Set in the world of elite professional tennis, and rooted in ancient Middle East hatreds of identity and blood loyalties, Basha is charged with the fiercely competitive nature of professional sports, and the dangers of terrorism. An already simmering Middle East begins to boil, and CIA Station Chief Grant Corbet must track down the highly successful terrorist, Basha, In a deadly race against time Grant hunts the illusive killer only to see his worst nightmare realized.

THE CORMORANT DOCUMENTS   Robert Middlemiss

Who is Cormorant, and why is his coded letter on Hitler's stationary found on a WWII Nazi bomber preserved in the Arctic? And why is the plane loaded with Goering's plundered are treasures? Mallory must find out or die. On the run from the British Secret Service and CIA, he finds himself caught in a secret that dates back to 1945.

CRISIS PENDING   Stephen Cornell

When U.S. oil refineries blow up, the White House and the Feds move fast, but not fast enough. Sherman Nassar Ramsey, terrorist for hire, a loner, brilliant, multilingual, and skilled with knives, pistols, and bare hands, moves around the country with contempt, ease and cunning.

As America's fuel system starts grinding to a halt, rioting breaks out for gasoline, and food becomes scarce, events draw Lee Hamilton's wife, Mary, into the crisis. And when Ramsey kidnaps her, the battle becomes very personal.

DANGER WITHIN   Mark Danielson

Over 100 feet down in cold ocean waters lies the wreck of pilot Kevin Hamilton's DC-10. In it are secrets which someone is desperate to keep. When the Navy sends a team of divers from the Explosives Ordinance Division, a mysterious explosion from the wreck almost destroys the salvage ship. The FBI steps in with Special Agent Mike Pentaglia. Track the life and death of Global Express Flight 3217 inside the gritty world of aviation, and discover the shocking cargo that was hidden on its last flight.

DEADLY ILLUMINATION   Serena Stier

It's summer 1890 in New York City. A ebullient young woman, Florence Tod, must challenge financier, John Pierpont Morgan, to solve a possible murder. J.P.'s librarian has ingested poison embedded in an illumination of a unique Hildegard van Bingen manuscript. Florence and her cousin, Isabella Stewart Gardner, discover the corpse. When Isabella secretly removes a gold tablet from the scene of the crime, she sets off a chain of events that will involve Florence and her in a dangerous conspiracy.

HOUR OF THE WOLVES   Stephane Daimlen-Völs

After more than three centuries, the *Poisons Affair* remains one of history's great, unsolved mysteries. The worst impulses of human nature—sordid sexual perversion,murderous intrigues, witchcraft, Satanic cults—thrive within the shadows of the Sun King's absolutism and will culminate in the darkest secret of his reign; the infamous *Poisons Affair*, a remarkably complex web of horror, masked by Baroque splendor, luxury and refinement.

A HOUSTON WEEKEND   Orville Palmer

Professor Edward Randall, not-yet-forty, divorced and separated from his daughters, is leading a solitary, cheerless existence in a university town. At a conference in Houston, he runs into his childhood sweetheart. Then she was poverty-stricken, American Indian. Now she's elegantly attired, driving an expensive Italian car and lives in a millionaires' enclave. Will their fortuitous encounter grow into anything meaningful?

JOHNNIE RAY AND MISS KILGALLEN   Bonnie Hearn Hill
                                                    and Larry Hill

Based on the real-life love affair between 1950's singer Johnnie Ray and columnist Dorothy Kilgallen. They had everything—wealth, fame, celebrity. The last thing they needed was love. *Johnnie Ray and Miss Kilgallen* is a love story that travels at a dangerous, roaring speed. Driven close to death from their excesses, both try to regain their lives and careers in a novel that goes beyond the bounds of mere biography.

THE LATERAL LINE   Robert Middlemiss

Kelly Travert was ready. She had the Israeli assassination pistol, she had coated the bullets with garlic, and tonight she would kill the woman agent who tortured and killed her father. When a negotiator for the CIA warns her, suddenly her father's death is not so simple anymore.

LEGACY OF A STAR   Peter Longley

Greed and murder run rampant—the prize: desert commerce of untold wealth, and the saving of the Jews. From the high temples to Roman barracks; from bat filled caves to magnificent villas on a sun-drenched sea; to the chamber of Salome, and the barren brothels where Esther rules, the Star moves across the heavens and men die—while a child is born.

LETHAL CURE   Kurt Popke

Dr. Jake Prescott is a resident on duty in the emergency room when medics rush in with a double trauma involving patients sustaining injuries during a home invasion. Jake learns that one patient is the intruder, the other, his wife, Sara. He also learns that his four-year-old daughter, Kelly, is missing, and his patient may hold the key to her recovery.

THE MEDUSA STRAIN   Chris Holmes

Finalist for *ForeWord Magazine's* 'Book of the Year'. A gripping tale of bio-terrorism that stunningly portrays the dangers of chemical warfare. Mohammed Ali Ossman, a bitter Iraqi scientist who hates America, breeds a deadly form of anthrax, and develops a diabolical means to initiate an epidemic. It is a story of personal courage in the face of terror, and of lost love found.

MR. IRRELEVANT   Jerry Marshall

Booklist Star Review. Chesty Hake, the last man chosen in the NFL draft, has been dubbed Mr. Irrelevant. By every yardstick, he should not be playing pro football, but because of his heart and high threshold for pain, he endures. Then during his eighth and final season, he slides into paranoia, and football will never be the same.

OPAL EYE DEVIL   John Hamilton Lewis

"Best historical thriller in decades." *Good Books.* In the age of the Robber Baron, *Opal Eye Devil* weaves an extraordinary tale about the brave men and women who risk everything as the discovery of oil rocks the world. The richness and pageantry of two great cultures, Great Britain and China, are brought together in a thrilling tale of adventure and human relationships.

PRIVATE JUSTICE   Richard Sand

Ben Franklin Award 'Best Mystery of the Year'. After taking brutal revenge for the murder of his twin brother, Lucas Rooks leaves the NYPD to become a private eye. A father turns to Rook to investigate the murder of his daughter. Rook's dark journey finds him racing to find the killer, who kills again and again as *Private Justice* careens toward a startling end.

ROADHOUSE BLUES   Baron R. Birtcher

From the sun-drenched sands of Santa Catalina Island to the smoky night clubs and back alleys of West Hollywood, Roadhouse Blues is a taut noir thriller. Newly retired Homicide detective Mike Travis is torn from the comfort of his chartered yacht business into the dark, bizarre underbelly of Los Angeles's music scene by a grisly string of murders.

RUBY TUESDAY   Baron R. Birtcher
When Mike Travis sails into the tropical harbor of Kona, Hawaii, he expects to put LA Homicide behind him. Instead, he finds the sometimes seamy back streets and dark underbelly of a tropical paradise and the world of music and high finance, where wealth and greed are steeped in sex, vengeance, and murder.

SAMSARA   John Hamilton Lewis
A thrilling tale of love and violence set in post-World War II Hong Kong. Nick Ridley, a captain in the RAF, is captured and sent to the infamous Japanese prisoner-of-war camp, Changi, in Singapore. He survives brutal treatment at the hands of the camp commandant, Colonel Tetsuro Matashima. Nick moves to Hong Kong, where he reunites with the love of his life, Courtney, and builds a world-class airline. On the eve of having his company recognized at the Crown Colony's official carrier, Courtney is kidnapped, and people begin to die. Nick is pulled into the quagmire, and must once again face the demon of Changi.

SECRET OF THE SCROLL   Chester D. Campbell
Finalist '*Deadly Dagger*' award, and *ForeWord Magazine's* 'Book of the Year' award. Deadly groups of Palestinians and Israelis struggle to gain possession of an ancient parchment that was unknowingly smuggled from Israel to the U.S. by a retired Air Force investigator. Col. Greg McKenzie finds himself mired in the duplicitous world of Middle East politics when his wife is taken hostage in an effort to force the return of the first-century Hebrew scroll.

SECRETS ARE ANONYMOUS   Frederick L. Cullen
A comic mystery with a cast of characters who weave multiple plots, puzzles, twists, and turns. A remarkable series of events unfold in the lives of a dozen residents of Bexley, Ohio. The journalism career of the principle character is derailed when her father shows up for her college graduation with his boyfriend on his way to a new life in California.

THE SEESAW SYNDROME   Michael Madden
A terrifying medical thriller that slices with a scalpel, exposing the greed and corruption that can happen when drug executives and medical researchers position themselves for huge profits. Biosense Pharmaceeuticals has produced a drug named Floragen, and now they need to test it on patients to gain FDA approval. But there's

a problem with the new drug. One of the side effects included death.

THE SERIAL KILLER'S DIET BOOK — Kevin Postupack

Finalist *ForeWord Magazine's* Book of the Year' award. Fred Orbis is fat, but he dreams of being Frederico Orbisini, internationally known novelist, existential philosopher, raconteur, and lover of women. Both a satire and a reflection on morals, God and the Devil, beauty, literature, and the best-seller-list, *The Serial Killer's Diet Book* is a delightful look at the universal human longing to become someone else.

THE STREET OF FOUR WINDS — Andrew Lazarus

Paris, just after World War II. A time for love, but also a time of political ferment. In the Left Bank section of the city, Tom Cortell, a tough, intellectual journalist, finally learns the meaning of love. Along with him is a gallery of fascinating characters who lead a merry and sometimes desperate chase between Paris, Switzerland, and Spain in search of themselves.

TUNNEL RUNNER — Richard Sand

A fast, deadly espionage thriller peopled with quirky and sometimes vicious characters, *Tunnel Runner* tells of a dark world where murder is committed and no one is brought to account, where loyalties exist side by side with lies and extreme violence.

WHAT GOES AROUND — Don Goldman

Finalist *ForeWord Magazine's* 'Book of the Year' award. Ray Banno, a medical researcher, was wrongfully incarcerated for bank fraud. *What Goes Around* is a dazzling tale of deception, treachery, revenge, and nonstop action that resolves around money, sex, and power. The book's sharp insight and hard-hitting style builds a high level of suspense as Banno strives for redemption.

DURBAN HOUSE NONFICTION

BEHIND THE MOUNTAIN: — Nick Williams
A CORPORATE SURVIVAL BOOK

A harrowing true story of courage and survival. Nick Williams is alone, and cut off in a blizzard behind the mountain. In order to survive, Nick called upon his training and experience that made him a highly-successful business executive. In *Behind the Mountain: A Corporate Survival Book*, you will fine d the finest practical advice on how to handle yourself in tough spots, be they life threatening to you, or threatening to your job performance or the company itself. Read and learn.

FISH HEADS, RICE, RICE WINE & WAR   LTC. Thomas G. Smith
(Ret.)

A human, yet humorous, look at the strangest and most misunderstood war ever, in which American soldiers were committed. Readers are offered an insiders view of American life in the midst of highly deplorable conditions, which often lead to laughter.

JIMMY CARTER AND THE RISE   Philip Pilevsky
OF MILITANT ISLAM

One of America's foremost authorities on the Middle East, Philip Pilevsky argues that President Jimmy Carter's failure to support the Shah of Iran led to the 1979 revolution. That revolution legitimized and provided a base of operations for militant Islamists across the Middle East. A most thought provoking book.

MIDDLE ESSENCE...   Landy Reed
WOMEN OF WONDER YEARS

A wonderful book by renowned speaker, Landy Reed that shows how real women in real circumstances have confronted and conquered the obstacles of midlife. This is a must have guide and companion to what can be the most significant and richest years of a woman's life.

PROTOCOL   Mary Jane McCaffree,
(25th Anniversary Edition)   Pauline Innis, and
        Richard Sand

Protocol is a comprehensive guide to proper diplomatic, official and social usage. The Bible for foreign governments, embassies, corporations, public relations firms, and individuals wishing to do business with the Federal Government. "A wealth of detail on every conceivable question, from titles and forms of address to ceremonies and flag etiquette." Department of State Newsletter.

SPORES, PLAGUES, HISTORY: Chris Holmes
THE STORY OF ANTHRAX

"Much more than the story of a microbe. It is the tale of history and prophecy woven into a fabric of what was, what might have been and what might yet be. What you are about to read is real—your are not in the Twilight Zone—adjusting your TV set will not change the picture. However, it is not hopeless, and we are not helpless. The same technology used to create biological weapons can protect us with better vaccines and treatments." CDR Ted J. Robinson, *U.S. Navy Epidemiologist.*

WHITE WITCH DOCTOR   John A. Hunt
A true story of life and death, hope and despair in apartheid-ruled South Africa.

White Witch Doctor details, white surgeon, John Hunt's fight to save his beloved country in a time of social unrest and political upheaval, drawing readers into the world of South African culture, mores and folkways, superstitions, and race relations.